"I didn't come he **of you,"** Fliss sai **"Nothing. I mean**

"Except my time," Saint noted dryly.

"Not even much of that," she assured him with a proud lift of her chin. "I'm catching the train back to Nottingham once I've finished the rest of my errands. You'll never hear from me again. But I had to tell you something that didn't feel right to send as a text."

"What's that?" He did his best to sound detached, but his ears were ringing with that word. *Never.* He held his breath, straining to hear over that jarring sound of a train disappearing down a tunnel. His muscles felt both paralyzed and tense with readiness to leap and catch.

"I'm pregnant."

Her Billion-Dollar Bump

DANI COLLINS

PRESENTS

Recycling programs
for this product may
not exist in your area.

ISBN-13: 978-1-335-59358-0

Her Billion-Dollar Bump

Harlequin Enterprises ULC
22 Adelaide St. West, 41st Floor
Toronto, Ontario M5H 4E3, Canada
www.Harlequin.com

Printed in Lithuania

MIX
Paper | Supporting
responsible forestry
FSC® C021394

Canadian **Dani Collins** knew in high school that she wanted to write romance for a living. Twenty-five years later, after marrying her high school sweetheart, having two kids with him, working at several generic office jobs and submitting countless manuscripts, she got The Call. Her first Harlequin novel won the Reviewers' Choice Award for Best First in Series from *RT Book Reviews*. She now works in her own office, writing romance.

Books by Dani Collins

Harlequin Presents

Innocent in Her Enemy's Bed
Awakened on Her Royal Wedding Night

Bound by a Surrogate Baby

The Baby His Secretary Carries
The Secret of Their Billion-Dollar Baby

Four Weddings and a Baby

Cinderella's Secret Baby
Wedding Night with the Wrong Billionaire
A Convenient Ring to Claim Her
A Baby to Make Her His Bride

Jet-Set Billionaires

Cinderella for the Miami Playboy

Visit the Author Profile page
at Harlequin.com for more titles.

This one is for Emmy Grayson and Maya Blake, my fellow authors in this trilogy. Thank you for being lovely and generous and a delight to work with.

PROLOGUE

As Felicity Corning picked up the wastebasket from beside the client's writing desk, a glint of gold script on glossy ebony caught her attention.

You are invited to attend London's premier Benefit for the Arts Gala

The gala was being held at a swanky art gallery in Chelsea two weeks from now.

This is the way, the devilish dreamer on her shoulder whispered. That voice was delusional, always telling her to *keep trying...find a way.*

Given how many obstacles the universe had put in her way, she was ready to throw in the towel on her fashion-design aspirations. She was only twenty-four, but after two years of knocking on fashion house doors that remained firmly closed, she was growing disheartened.

She understood that dropping out of her degree—and having books and books of sketches with only a few physical samples—meant she wasn't seen as a viable candidate for even an unpaid intern position. The designers needed to see more commitment to her craft, but she couldn't help feeling like she had already missed the boat.

If you could show them what you're capable of, the voice persisted, *someone might finally take you seriously.*

"No," she said aloud.

Risking her current job was not the way to go about it. Housekeeping might not be the most glamorous job in the world, but the agency catered to wealthy clients. That was why she had taken it. She often got to put away samples, shopping, and dry cleaning from top designers. Aside from the occasional post-party apocalypse, the work was basic and physical but undemanding. The pay covered her bills. More or less. London was obscenely expensive.

Felicity actually lived a penurious existence. Most artists did. She didn't mind going without lattes or streaming services so she could spend her scant disposable income on bolts of silk and high-end notions, though. Building out her collection was her way forward. It was her passion. It was the only entertainment she needed.

However, her life had fallen into a rut. Every day was a grind that only seemed to entrench her deeper into a place she didn't want to be. She had been thinking of going back to school to finish her degree, which she had waffled her way through the first time round. She had been persuaded by her grandmother into thinking a practical business degree was the way to go, then later switched to visual arts before knocking off to take care of Granny until she had passed away.

Going back to school would create the Catch-22 of having no time outside of her classes and day job to sew. Plus, most fashion houses were looking for a post-graduate degree. It would be years before she was remotely "qualified" in the eyes of top designers.

With a sigh of frustration, Felicity carried the wastebasket into the housekeeping closet, but she didn't immediately empty it into the larger bin. First, she plucked out the invitation and set it on the shelf of cleaning products.

She wasn't *taking* it, she told her squirming conscience. She was merely not throwing it away.

Maybe the owner of this three-bedroom townhome—a well-known supermodel—had tossed it by accident. She had recently been cast in a blockbuster movie and was out of town. That was likely why she had discarded the invitation despite the message on the back.

Delia Chevron and date, courtesy of Brightest Star Studio

The studio must have picked up the ticket price for her. How nice to be so rich and famous you could throw away a dinner worth a few hundred pounds. Such a waste. A crime, really, when good people went hungry every day.

People like you, the voice whispered.

"Shut up," she hissed.

But when Felicity left for the day, she told herself she was only taking the card as inspiration. Someday *she* would be invited to an event like this—or one of her gowns would, she thought wryly.

But she knew better. She knew she would take a risk that could go horribly awry.

On the other hand, it could change her life.

As it turned out, it did both.

CHAPTER ONE

SAINT MONTGOMERY WOULD have been ushered down the red carpet with or without a date, but he was solo tonight, so he chose the less conspicuous side entrance where he was funneled like a steer for branding past a thinner bank of photographers. He couldn't avoid the barrage of questions on his recent breakup, however.

"Saint! Are you and Julie still speaking? What happened?"

He should have brought a date. A new face would have changed the narrative, and God knew he was tired of this one.

Historically, his romantic liaisons were casual and pleasant and ended without conflict. If asked about a particular breakup, he would claim "artistic differences" or some other facetious explanation.

His affair with Julie, however, was the gift that kept on giving. Or taking, as it turned out.

He'd caught her trying to break into his laptop. She'd claimed to be the jealous type who'd suspected him of an affair. He had assured her he was the possessive type, especially when it came to his proprietary software.

Saint wasn't surprised she'd had a mercenary motive in

sleeping with him. Most people operated in their own self-interest, including him, but this experience had shaken his already jaded view of his fellow human beings.

When he had begun seeing Julie, he had taken her at face value, believing she hadn't needed anything from him beyond affluent companionship. She was the daughter of a famous sportscaster in the US and stood to inherit millions. She had recently broken up with a star athlete and had told Saint she wasn't ready for anything serious again. She wanted marriage and children "someday" but not today. She had fit seamlessly into his social circle of tycoons and celebrities, flirting and charming wherever she'd gone.

She had seemed an even match for Saint, who always promised monogamy, but little else. He had dropped his guard more than he normally would, never suspecting that Julie had a gambling addiction. Or that she would attempt industrial espionage to pay down her debts.

She could have cost him billions if his bespoke security software hadn't alerted him to her attempt to clone it. He hadn't pressed charges. He'd gone easy on her, expelling her from his life while offering to pay for a treatment program.

She had petulantly refused, then gone on every damned talk show in the English-speaking world, literally selling a tale that *he* had wronged *her*.

This story was well past its shelf life. Saint was beyond ready to change the channel.

"You can wait for your party over there." Ahead of him, the greeter waved a woman into purgatory on the far side of the single door and invited the group ahead of him to come forward.

A kick of desire arrested him as he ate up the vision in blue.

Who was she? She wasn't the most beautiful woman he'd ever seen. More eye-catching in an undiscovered, wall-flower way. Most women had arrived dressed to compete with plunging necklines and tiaras and capes made of os-trich feathers. This one's makeup was muted. Her brunette hair fell in subtle waves from a side part. Rather than an ice cap's worth of diamonds, she wore a pair of gold hoops and a thin chain with a locket. Her gown was a simple halter style that tied behind her neck before cradling her ample breasts in soft gathers above a high, wide waistband. The skirt fell in a solid curtain off her wide hips, leaving her legs and shoes hidden.

He let his gaze return to those lovely breasts sitting heavy and relaxed in the gathered cups of silk. No bra. He would swear it on his life. Her nipples were leaving a sub-tle impression beneath the sheen of fabric. One soft swell lifted and moved without restraint as she brushed her hair back from her cheek.

He swallowed. Saint was a healthy man with a strong sexual appetite, but he rarely felt need. Not like this. Not hunger that was immediate and intense and specific.

Her unease was palpable as she pressed a self-conscious smile onto her lips and eyed the bank of photographers. They were ignoring her in favor of new arrivals at the end of the line.

Wait. Was she looking for a path of escape? She pressed her lips together and took a step.

"Angel," Saint said on impulse, stepping toward her. "I'm

so glad you decided to come." He crooked his arm in invitation, aware of the cameras shifting to the pair of them.

"What?" Her amber gaze flashed to Saint, hitting him like a shot of whiskey, sending even more heat pouring into his gut and out to his extremities. The delicious warmth sank to pool low and heavy behind his fly. It was exciting. Dangerous, but exciting.

"Sir." The greeter reacted to Saint trying to bypass him, then stammered, "I beg your pardon, Mr. Montgomery. Of course you may go in."

"We're blocking the entrance," Saint said, steadying his new date's faltering steps as he guided her into the noisy foyer, then found them a quiet corner in the main gallery.

She blinked, taking in the freestanding sculptures and abstract oils surrounding tables placed like stepping stones into the labyrinth of the gallery's showrooms. The glitterati milled in pockets at the edges. Above them, origami flowers were suspended on threads, drifting and bobbing on gentle, unseen currents, like an upside-down meadow.

The woman's enchantment was cute, her uptilted mouth in that rosy pink nearly irresistible.

"I was stood up, too," Saint said, signaling a server to bring champagne.

"You're joking." Her wide-eyed gaze came down from the ceiling as she took the glass he handed her.

"Prevaricating," he admitted. No one would ever leave him waiting. "I parted ways with my date two weeks ago."

"I'm so sorry." She sounded sincere, which was adorable.

"It's for the best. And you? Who had the poor taste to leave you hanging?"

"Are we prevaricating?" Her chin dropped in a sly, self-deprecating dip. "I actually knew my…um…date wouldn't be here. I came anyway, hoping they'd let me in, which they didn't. So you've aided and abetted a party crasher." She wrinkled her nose.

"I've done worse."

She started to say something, then checked herself, biting her lips with contrition.

"What? You've heard that about me?" That was no surprise. He'd misspent his young adult years on wine, women and song. He was a lot more circumspect these days, but that playboy reputation remained his calling card and had its uses, so he didn't fight it.

"Maybe." Her lashes flickered as her gaze traveled across the unpadded shoulders of his jacket and down to the buttons that closed it.

He stole the opportunity to take another long drink of her figure-eight figure—which was a solid ten. He came back in time to see the tip of her tongue slide along the seam of her lips.

Her bottom lip was wide and full, the top one thinner with two sharp peaks in the center and an uptilt at the corners that gave an impression she had an amusing secret.

Damn, but he wanted to kiss her. Right. Now.

But when her gaze lifted to his, there was wariness behind the speculation. She quirked a quizzical brow at him.

"Are you really Saint Montgomery?"

"Yes." He liked his name in her accent. It wasn't one of those posh pronunciations that scolded, demanding he behave like his namesake. Her broad inflection held a rueful skepticism that seemed to know he was the furthest thing from a saint.

"So why are you talking to me?"

He liked how direct she was, too. "Is that a real question? I find you attractive."

She choked on the sip of champagne she'd started to take. "No." She tilted her head, eyeing him with suspicion. "At best, you're on a rebound from your recent breakup."

He winced, caught, but, "Both things can be true, can't they? I do find you attractive, but it also suited me to give the paparazzi fresh meat to chew on. Now they're out there wondering who the hell I came in with."

Her eyes widened with alarm.

"Why does that worry you? Who *did* I come in with?"

"I'd rather not say." She glanced around and shook her head with something like incredulity. "I was misrepresenting myself by turning up here and really need to quit while I'm ahead. Thank you for getting me in, but I'm leaving."

"Why?" He put out a hand, needing to touch her again if only to graze her bare elbow. And watch her nipples peak against the thin silk of her gown. "Who was your date? Why did you come if you didn't think they'd let you in?"

"I'm embarrassed to say. Genuinely." Her flush of awareness turned to dark pink stains on her cheeks. Her bright-eyed amusement was very much at her own expense. "I'll do more damage than good if I stick around, so… It was nice to meet you, but I have to go. Even though it *galls* me to walk away from a dinner worth a hundred pounds."

She really was new here. "It's twenty-five thousand."

"What is? This statue?" She halted herself from setting her unfinished glass on the base of a nearby sculpture.

"The plate fee."

"Is twenty-five thousand pounds?" she cried and fumbled her glass, splashing champagne against her knuckles. She added an earthy epithet that he would've loved to hear against his ear while they were between the sheets.

He offered his pocket square, not bothering to mention he'd underwritten a table of ten for his London team of executives and their spouses.

"I'm definitely leaving," she blurted as she handed back his damp square of silk.

"Not before midnight, Cinderella," he cajoled, caressing her arm again, liking how quickly goose bumps rose against his tickling touch. He nodded toward an archway into another room. "I have to make the rounds. Stay and amuse me."

She sobered. "I don't mind laughing at myself, but I don't care to become entertainment for others."

"Why would you be?" He frowned.

"We can both tell I'm out of my league here," she said with reproach. "Why else would you want me on your arm? Social anxiety?"

"I find your sense of humor a welcome balance to people who take themselves far too seriously."

"Gosh, fun as it sounds to meet those people, I'll have to give it a miss." She handed her glass to a passing server.

A lurching sensation pulled in his chest. He wanted to catch at her as though she was falling off a cliff away from him.

"Saint Montgomery. Just the man I need." A woman's hand arrived on his shoulder. She was the forty-something wife of a man Saint had met somewhere for some reason. Her chestnut hair was piled atop her head, her gown a racy haute-couture creation that framed cleavage where a ruby the size of a holiday turkey nested. "I'm planning an eclipse party. I need your clever brain to calculate the perfect time and place. Hello. You're not Julie."

His mystery woman froze like a bunny, then produced a dazzling smile that hit Saint like a ball of sunshine even though it was directed at the other woman.

"I'm not Julie, you're right. I'm Fliss. Sadly, you've missed this year's total eclipse. There will be another in about fourteen months with good views from Iceland, Portugal and Spain. The path is easy enough to find online. I would look it up for you, but I've been called away, so… um…good night." She included Saint in her wave of departure.

"Don't be silly, Fliss. I can't leave you to find your own way home." What a flossy, fluttery name. It suited her perfectly. "Excuse us."

Saint flashed a dismissive smile at the other woman, who was watching them with great curiosity, and steered Fliss against the tide of people still streaming in.

"You don't have to leave. You'll miss a dinner worth a fraction of what you paid for it." Fliss rolled her eyes as they emerged into the press of people still hovering and hurrying through the dusk.

A cool spring breeze slithered through the crowd, ruffling into his collar and dancing against her loose hair.

"You're missing dinner, too. We'll have to find somewhere else to eat." He texted his driver.

"I was being sarcastic. I'll—"

"Saint! Who's your date?" A photographer waiting near the curb began flashing their bulb at them, drawing others to do the same.

Fliss sent an appalled look to Saint.

"Ignore them." He glanced at a muscled security guard wearing an earpiece and a black T-shirt.

The bouncer immediately turned himself into a bulwark against the photographers, opening his arms wide and forcing the photographers back.

"Hey! What's your name? How long have you been dating Saint?"

Fliss was still staring at him with horror.

"There's my car." His driver was coming in on the far side, against the arrival lane, but both directions were clogged with traffic.

He caught her hand and slipped between two limos dispensing passengers, then opened the rear door where his driver had paused in the middle of the street. Saint swept the hem of her gown into the car and slammed the door, then circled to the other side.

"What's going to happen now?" Fliss asked, twisting to look through the rear window as their car crept forward.

"Now I don't have to spend the next three hours talking about astrology. Thank you."

She blinked once at him, then settled into her seat, nose forward. "And here I was about to ask for your sign."

"Scorpio," he drawled. "I only remember because someone told me once that it explains my sting."

"I can see that." She slid him a side-eye. "Bold to the point of fearless. Intense. Likes to be in charge. Did you know that Scorpios secretly believe in astrology?"

"Untrue."

"Well, it wouldn't be a secret if you admitted it, would it?" Amusement twitched the sharp corners of her mouth.

"I'm going to be sorry I ever met you, aren't I?" He wasn't. This was the most fun he'd had in ages.

"Don't worry. Our acquaintance will be very brief." She craned her neck, looking past the driver to the heavy traffic ahead. "After you get me out of here, you'll never see me again."

"I'll have to make the most of my time with you, then. Won't I, Fliss?"

CHAPTER TWO

THE INTIMATE WAY he said her name raised goose bumps all over her body. In fact, he'd been doing that to her from the moment he'd called her Angel and swept her into the gallery.

Fliss knew it was deliberate on his part. She knew who Saint Montgomery was. Or, at least, she knew what the headlines said about him. He was the heir to Grayscale Technologies, one of Silicon Valley's pillars of wealth and innovation. He held a prestigious position within the company, but whether he did actual work was anyone's guess. He was far more well-known for his jet-setting lifestyle and rotating bevy of beautiful women.

He was a player and seemed to want to play with her.

Much to her chagrin, she was allowing it.

Fliss knew better, but every time she looked at him, her brain shorted out. How could it not? He was gorgeous! Rather than the standard tuxedo most men had donned, Saint wore a dark blue jacket with geometric patterns embroidered into it. His black silk lapels framed his black silk tie against a crisp white shirt. His perfectly tailored trousers landed precisely on his glossy black shoes, and none of it distracted from his ruggedly handsome features. In fact, it only accentuated his athletic physique and sheer charisma.

His straight, dark brows gave him a stern look that reached all the way into the pit of her belly, but the hint of curl in his dirty blond hair, and the stubble that framed his sensually full mouth, were pure hedonism.

Don't stare, she reminded herself, but he really was as good-looking in person as he was in photos. More. He had an aura of lazy confidence that was positively magnetic.

The way his gaze slid over her like a caress was dark magic that ought to have sent her tucking and rolling from the car, not sitting here holding her breath, waiting to see what would happen next.

Just go home.

Coming to the art gallery had been a terrible idea. She had traded away shifts and distressed her credit card to make this gown in time, and it hadn't held up against the ones by the professionals. Not at all. It was fine for a brides-maid at a country wedding, but her belief that its simplic-ity was classic had actually been a fear-based decision. She saw that now.

Which, she supposed, meant the night wasn't a total waste of time. *You learn more from failure than success*, Granny used to say. Fliss understood now why she and her work weren't being taken seriously. Insecurity was holding her back from expressing herself.

Her confidence had taken a major hit when she'd ar-rived and seen how outgunned she was. Rather than try for the red carpet, she'd slinked into the queue for the side entrance only to be shuffled to the side because she wasn't the invitee.

She had been ready to go home, tail between her legs, when this ridiculously famous man had swept her into the party, then into his car, and now—

"My hotel," he told the driver as traffic began to clear.

Such a playboy.

"Presumptuous," she cast at him before leaning forward to say to the driver, "You can drop me at the nearest tube station."

"For *dinner*. You're the one making presumptions," Saint said indignantly, but laughter twitched his lips.

Amusement tickled inside her chest along with flutters of excitement and intrigue. Was he really this superficial and predictable? Or was there more to him? She wanted to know.

And she *would* rather catch a car-share from a hotel than have him drop her outside the humble row house where she rented a room with four other housemates. Also, she had skipped lunch because she'd been pressed for time and had thought she would be eating well tonight.

Was she rationalizing spending more time with him? Absolutely.

Was she also giving in to that ambitious, calculating part of herself that had gone so far as to put on her own gown and turn up with Delia Chevron's invitation in her handbag, trying to blag her way into a world where she didn't belong?

How had she deluded herself into believing she could be "discovered" on the red carpet? Talk about the ultimate queue jumper!

She was mortified by her own behavior and grateful she'd slipped away without anyone knowing her name. She had only provided her nickname to that woman who'd called her "not Julie." If Granny were alive to hear about this, Felicity would feel the old woman's yardstick, for sure. She'd have opinions about Fliss allowing a serial woman-izer like Saint Montgomery to take her to dinner, too.

You'll know the right man when you meet him, Granny's voice had assured her countless times. *Don't waste time with boys who don't appreciate you.*

Fliss had been schooled rather harshly on how disre-spectful a boy could be. Saint reminded her a lot of that first and only boyfriend, emanating the same alpha qualities of strength and wealth and handsome popularity.

Fliss knew better than to imagine he was the Mr. Right she was waiting for, but this felt like a chance at something— not fame or gain, but connection. She couldn't pinpoint why it felt so necessary to spend a little more time with him, but when they exited the car outside his hotel, she didn't refuse his dinner invitation and order a car to take her home.

She entered the door the uniformed doorman held for her, aware of Saint's hand in her lower back as he came in right behind her.

The hotel was one that she had only ever heard of as being very posh. She tried not to gawk, but it was like some-thing out of a movie with its checkered tiles and chande-liers, its arches and columns and refined opulence.

The staff treated Saint like a movie star, too. Or, she sup-posed, like a man who could buy out the place if he wanted to. As they arrived at the dining room, the maître d' escorted them to a table that bore a Reserved sign, leaving a well-dressed party of four grumbling at the reception podium.

"Do you have any allergies?" Saint asked Fliss as he seated her.

"No."

"Have the chef prepare us a tasting menu," he told the maître d'. "Wine to pair, and don't let anyone bother us."

The man nodded with deference and melted away.

"Fliss. Is that short for something?" Saint unbuttoned his jacket as he sat, leaving it hanging open while he leaned back, at ease with who he was and where they were. "Tell me about yourself."

Ugh. "Must I?"

"You don't want to?" His gaze delved deep into her own.

"It's gloomy." She dropped her own gaze, heart clenching. "My parents died when I was eight. They were all I had aside from my granny. She raised me and passed a couple of years ago. I moved to London for a fresh start." Losing her was still a painful knife in her chest.

"I'm sorry for your loss."

"Thanks."

An amuse-bouche arrived to lighten the mood. It was a single bite of ceviche on a foam of fragrant dill served on a silver spoon, topped by a few grains of caviar and a sprinkle of chopped chive. They chased it with a light wine ripe with notes of pear and anise.

Fliss had never noticed such subtleties of flavor before. She thought her senses might've been sharpened by the company she was in. Being in the aura of this man was a thrill somewhere between lion taming and steering a high-performance car through the streets of Monaco.

"What do you do here?" he asked.

"Fashion designer." It might not have been her job, but painters were artists even if they didn't sell their work. "I'm still starting out. You? What brings you to London?"

"Patting the backs of our top performers at the gala this evening."

"Shouldn't you be there, then?"

He shrugged it off. "They'll have more fun without the boss keeping them in check."

"Is that what your work entails? Travel and glad-handing?"

"Much of it, yes." His eyes narrowed with suspicion. "Why are you asking about my work?"

"Why are you interested in mine? We have to talk about something. It's too bad I don't have my tarot cards." She looked to her small handbag. "I could have done a reading for you."

"Do you really believe in the supernatural, or are you stringing me along?"

"Both." She couldn't help grinning. "Granny used to take me to a psychic sometimes, to see if we could talk to my parents. When I was twelve, I won my tarot cards at a fair. It came with a book of interpretations, so I spent the rest of my adolescence learning to read them. I've delved a little into astrology and numerology. Crystals. As far as explaining life's mysteries, they make as much sense as anything else."

"What about ghosts?"

"What about them? Don't say you don't believe in them." She leaned forward to warn, "There's one right behind you."

It was their server, coming to remove their plates. Saint's reaction to the sudden movement in his periphery was a flicker of his gaze, then a shake of his head at her. "You're trouble."

She bit back a chuckle, enjoying herself. This was a unique position. She had no history with him, no future—

only now. It allowed her to be completely herself without fear of judgment or consequence. It was thrilling.

"I know how farfetched these things sound," she conceded. "But belief isn't about being rational, is it? It's what we convince ourselves is true when we don't have evidence to tell us otherwise. When I set out my cards, that's all I'm looking for—evidence to support a belief I already have. Should I move to London? Oh, look. I pulled a card that means material success. That must mean I'll achieve my goals if I move to London."

"Sounds more like you're tricking yourself."

"We all trick ourselves." Fliss waved that away. "If you prefer to believe that heaven exists, that's the trick you've chosen because there's no way to prove what really happens after death. Maybe it's my imagination that I hear my grandmother's voice when I set out my cards, but who cares if it is? It brings me comfort to feel like I'm talking to her. And in a way, I *am* keeping her spirit alive by invoking her. Does that make her a ghost whose energy is in the room?"

"You've almost convinced me to believe in something completely illogical." He tilted his head as though trying to understand how she'd accomplished it. "It sounds like you were very close with her."

"I was." She was unable to prevent the pang of loss that thinned her voice. "But her quality of life had deteriorated so much by the time she passed, I really believe she's in a better place. It was still hard to be left behind." She could feel herself descending into melancholy so she added, "She loved to spin a yarn, too. You couldn't trust a word she said. I suppose I keep her alive in that way as well."

Saint's face blanked. "Is everything you've just told me pure BS?"

"Does it matter? You wanted to be entertained, and you are. Thank you." She smiled as the server presented a crystal shot glass filled with layers of gazpacho from dark red beet through a rich green cucumber and avocado to a bright yellow heirloom tomato topped with a morsel of lobster and a sprig of mint.

A Reuilly Sauvignon Blanc was poured into a fresh glass, even though she hadn't finished her first glass of wine and the bottle was still mostly full.

Saint wasn't trying to get her drunk by urging her to finish, though. He caught her concerned glance at the ice bucket and said drily, "The staff won't let the opened bottles go to waste."

The soup was gone in three swallows but left a minty tang on Fliss's tongue that was amplified by a sip of the citrus and vanilla in the wine.

They talked about incidentals over a delicate bouquet of colorful baby lettuce leaves and sprigs of herbs arranged with edible flowers on a pureed dressing, then a main of braised duck with baby turnips and figs.

Saint seemed genuinely interested in her, asking about her taste in music and movies, where she had traveled— London and a school trip to Paris, years ago. He made her feel special, but Fliss knew that was an illusion. She was *here*. That was all.

It was still nice to be on a date. She had a strong sense of self and what she wanted to accomplish with her life, but she suffered certain feelings of inadequacy and lack of experience with romantic relationships.

She veered from thinking about that piece-of-dirt boyfriend she'd had back in sixth form, irritated that she was still letting him affect her, but he'd made sexuality such a complicated thing for her. At first, it had been fun and light, but soon he'd pressured her to have sex. She'd gone along with it out of insecurity with their relationship and normal adolescent curiosity, but it had been very un-special.

First times were often awkward, so she wouldn't have had such hard feelings about it, but he'd begun telling people she'd given it up to him. Angry, she'd broken up with him only for him to spread nasty rumors that he'd broken things off because she was "the town bike."

She'd lost friendships over it and a lot of trust in boys. For the rest of school and into uni, she had had all the typical curiosity and desires of a healthy, youthful person, but she'd also felt deeply self-conscious when she'd showed so much as a collarbone or an ankle, loath to draw sexual attention in case she'd been accused of asking for it.

Eventually, she'd begun to relax and come out of her shell again, but by then, Granny's health had turned. Fliss had moved home, where she had fallen back into old patterns of keeping her head down. In a lot of ways, worry for Granny had tapped her out emotionally, too. There hadn't been room for a romantic relationship, so she hadn't pursued any.

Moving to London had been another fresh start, but between making ends meet and chasing her dreams, she didn't have much time for a social life. Occasionally, she joined her housemates at the pub, but she'd never met a man who interested her enough to choose him over her ambitions.

Until now.

DANI COLLINS   29

Not that Saint was likely to derail her in any way. He was the most unattainable man in dating history. It was well-documented. He was buying her dinner. That was all this was and all it would be.

She turned the tables on him, though, and learned that his parents lived in New York and that he had a penthouse there but also a home in California because he spent so much time there. He attended plays or movie *premieres*. He was wired for logic and technology where she gravitated to arts and the ethereal. He traveled the globe on a monthly basis.

"We genuinely have nothing in common," Fliss noted wryly. "I have a passport I've used precisely once. I renewed it when I moved to London, hoping I'd need it for work." Surely she would be recognized as a genius and sent to Fashion Week in New York? Or, at the very least, would book herself a trip to attend?

"What about dancing?" He glanced to where couples were stepping and turning in tempo to the pianist's romantic melody.

"Are you asking if I'm any good? Not really. I'm guessing you're an expert?"

"I am." He rose and held out his hand in invitation.

"At least we're both humble," she teased, but he had every right to his arrogance. Everything about him shortened her breath in the most delicious way.

Since when did she find a man's hand sexy? The glimpse of his inner wrist above his wide palm and long fingers seemed like the most erotic peek of skin in the world. Fliss wanted to kiss that spot where his skin was a shade less tanned than the rest.

Warming with a blush, she set her hand in his, feeling drawn upward by an unseen force. Pulled and gathered and spun onto a cloud even though her feet weren't yet on the dance floor.

As they arrived, Saint drew her into his arms and her body became a flame, hot and bright and insubstantial.

Then she embarrassed herself by bumping straight into him. As her curves mashed up against his firm, strong body, her stomach swooped and plummeted.

"I'm sorry! See? I'm bad at this."

"Listen to the music. Let me lead." His voice was low and hypnotic. "Trust me."

She didn't trust him. Or shouldn't. But she had quit listening to the voice of caution and now began to feel. The piano notes filled her ears, but she could swear she heard his heartbeat at a deeper level, matching hers. All of her became synchronized to him. The breadth of his shoulders blocked out the rest of the room, making him her world. The faint trace of aftershave against his throat filled her nostrils, and his hand cradling hers sent warmth penetrating into her bloodstream.

The sure way he advanced and retreated, moving her with ease as she gave herself up to his mastery reinforced her sense of belonging to him. Of becoming an extension of him.

This is the one.

The voice that spoke wasn't angel or devil or Granny. It was her deepest voice of intuitive knowledge. Despite all the evidence to the contrary, a fine vibration within her was harmonizing with his. Fliss gave herself up to it as they moved. Neither of them was leading or following. They were in perfect alignment.

This was how it would feel to make love with him, she understood as sensuality unfurled inside her. Natural and easy. She didn't need her precious tarot cards to tell her he'd be good at sex, either. He'd draw her effortlessly down a path of iniquity, and she would love every second of it.

"What's funny?" Saint murmured, making her realize he was looking at her.

"This situation. It's very surreal to me," she admitted, trying to hide the blush that betrayed where her thoughts had strayed. "It must be very common for you, though? Picking up women?"

There was a flash behind his eyes. Insulted?

He directed his attention over her head, releasing a noise of disparagement. "Women do the picking up. I simply allow it."

"I guess I'm a natural. I didn't realize that's what I was doing." *Was* that what she had been doing?

Their gazes clashed again. This time the flash in his eyes was lightning that struck all the way into the pit of her belly and lower, leaving a scorch in her loins. A certain apprehension washed over her, too. It was the wild combination of exhilaration and fear when tasting nature's raw power. Of being overwhelmed by it.

"It is me this time," he said in that smoky voice that made her skin feel tight.

Picking her up? He was more than a natural at it. He was a world-class wizard.

"I thought this was only dinner?" She dropped her gaze

to the knot in his tie, trying to hide the flare of temptation that came into her eyes.

He probably read her temptation in her tension and the telltale blush that was warming her cheeks.

"It can be, if that's what you prefer." Was there tension in him, too? Her ears were straining to take in every tiny signal between them. "But I like to take my fate into my own hands, rather than rely on the stars to offer me what I want." His mouth curled at the corner. "If there's a chance for more than dinner, I'd like to seize it."

He'd like to seize her, too, apparently, given how his grip tightened slightly on her waist and hand.

Before Fliss realized what he was doing, he guided her away from him in a slow spin that was unexpected enough to make her dizzily catch onto him when she came back into his arms. Then he dipped her slightly over his arm, so she was off-balance, and lowered his head.

He stopped before he kissed her. His whispered "Is there?" wafted across her lips. "A chance?"

Oh, dear.

Her heart was thudding in a mix of anxiety and excitement, and her hands were holding tight to him—because she was literally off-balance. She could have shaken him off and stood on her own two feet rather than let him hold her tipped like this, but her brain had short-circuited again. All she was really aware of was his mouth, right there, filling her with such yearning she could hardly breathe.

She lifted her chin in welcome, offering her mouth to him.

The lightest of touches brushed her lips. A subtle rest of lips to lips. A greeting. Not even a dalliance. He waited for her to make the slight shift and find the angle that fit their mouths together more fully.

Then he rocked his head, a request. *Invite me.*

She did, sighing as his arm grew more firm around her and his tongue probed in a languorous quest. When the tip of his tongue brushed the roof of her mouth, feathery caresses seemed to scroll over her whole body from nape to tailbone, down her arms and legs and high between her thighs, into that pulsing, throbbing place that she'd been trying to ignore but felt heavy and flooded with heat. With longing.

She gasped at the startling way he brought her whole body to life, but he only deepened their kiss, as though seeking whatever she might be holding back from him. Chasing. Demanding.

Fliss had known she wasn't his match financially or socially, but she had been pretending they were equals in a more esoteric way. Wit, perhaps. Or in their lighthearted detachment from this dinner of theirs.

This kiss, however. This kiss demonstrated just how far out of her league she really was. It was a plunge from thirty-thousand feet into thin air. It knocked the breath from her lungs, leaving her ears rushing with nothing but the scream of wind.

His lips raked across hers in an unbridled claim that shook apart all she'd ever known about kissing, which was admittedly a lot less than she'd realized. He cupped the back of her head, and the stubble on his jaw grazed her chin.

When a whimper resounded in her throat, he drew her upright, but desperation had her winding her arms around his neck. *Don't stop.* She stood on tiptoe and pressed herself harder to him. She wanted to be closer. Closer still.

He growled and crushed her to his front and nipped at her bottom lip before soothing and suckling, causing more lightning to strike through her abdomen and into her sex. More trickles of need and more shivers of ecstatic pleasure traveled down her spine.

Very dimly, she was aware that they were in public, that they should stop, but she couldn't make herself pull away. She tasted wine and traces of clove and inhaled a fading aftershave that would remain imprinted on her senses forever.

Her eyelids had fluttered closed. All that existed was this dark enveloping sense of the world having fallen away. She knew only distant sensations of satin and embroidered wool. Her fingertips found the line where his cool hair cut a precise line against the hot skin at the back of his neck. She was aware of her breasts being crushed against the plane of his chest in a way that was a relief but increased the yearning within her. His hard thighs warmed the fall of her skirt against the front of her legs, and his hand drew a slow, lazy circle in her lower back that was as promising as it was proprietary.

This was what she had been waiting for in her ambivalence toward dating. Not commitment or Mr. Right but this rush of desire that pulsed inside her like a drum beat. Like an imperative.

She had been waiting for a man to kiss her as though she was essential to him. That was how she felt when he started to draw back, then returned as though he couldn't resist one more long, thorough, greedy taste.

He lifted his head and kept her in the shelter of his arms.

She was trembling and grateful for his support. Her knees were gelatin, the rest of her soft as melted wax. His hand was tucked beneath her hair, cupping the back of her neck, thumb moving in a restless, soothing caress against her nape. The other held her body pressed close enough to feel the rapid tattoo of his heart through the layer of his jacket and the thick shape of his erection against her stomach.

They were drawing attention. She covered her burning lips with her crooked finger.

When she stepped out of his arms, he slid his hand down her bare shoulder, leaving a wake of tingles before he buttoned his jacket to disguise the effect she'd had on him.

As they arrived back at their table, he picked up her handbag. "Do you want to stay for dessert or bring it to my room?"

"I—"

Don't, she warned herself.

But that deep, inner, intuitive voice said, *He's the one*.

Her voice was thick as honey. "I'm sure the staff won't let it go to waste if we skip it."

Rather than the smug smile she'd expected, his cheek ticked. He took her hand as they left the restaurant.

CHAPTER THREE

MOST PEOPLE ASSUMED Saint was a risk junkie. Or at the very least, someone who didn't care about risks so long as he got what he wanted.

That wasn't true at all. As a child, he had learned to calculate risk very quickly. If he'd wanted to speak to his father, he'd first weighed whether the subject was worth his father's wrath at having his work interrupted. If he'd tried out for the school play, would it be worth his mother showing up tipsy and making it about her?

Later, when he and his father had found common ground in programming and hardware, his mother had been hurt and jealous. Which would he rather endure? His mother's heartbreak or his father's belittling lecture?

Those early consequences had prepared him for the perils in later relationships: the friend who was only a friend because he wanted access to the newest smart phone, or the girl who liked his money more than she liked him, or the people who invited him to parties to elevate their own social standing.

Saint was always aware when people were trying to use him. He often allowed it. There were silver linings: business advantages, amusing entertainments. Sex.

But he had taught those around him to expect very little from him beyond a sarcastic remark and that he would pick up the bill.

This woman beside him in the elevator, with her quirky sense of humor and understated beauty and fiery depths of passion, felt like a gamble he ought to take more time to calculate. His reaction to her was too sharp. Too intense. That kiss had been so hot, so all encompassing, he'd been seared from hairline to toenails.

This wasn't purely a carnal reaction, though. That was the part making his nerve endings sting with danger. He'd been drawn to her all night—from the first glimpse to his compulsion to leave the gala with her. To learn more about her. To touch her.

She was as puzzling as she was alluring. Both open and closed. That air of mystery, with her refusing to give him her full name, tickled at his well-strung trip wires, but what damage could she possibly do to him if they spent the night together? He didn't have anything in his room that he wasn't prepared to lose. He weathered bad publicity like a seasonal storm.

Hell, he was in a small storm right now, he recalled with annoyance, but that fiasco with Julie reminded him to make clear to Fliss that this evening had its limits.

"I'm due in New York first thing in the morning," he said. "I'll be leaving for the airport in a few hours, but stay the night. Use the room tomorrow if you want. Visit the spa."

The gold in her irises tarnished slightly before she blinked it away. "I have to work tomorrow." Her mouth twitched. "But you've very good at this. Very smooth." She looked down to where she held her purse and gave its clasp a few nervous clicks. "I've always wondered how these things were handled. By that I mean, um, I don't have condoms." She peeked up at him in question.

"I do." Always. There was one in his pocket that he'd pulled from his stash out of habit.

Fliss nodded, but her brows pulled into a frown of consternation.

"Second thoughts? That's fine." He might actually die if she changed her mind, though. He'd never felt horniness like this. So specific. So beastly. Like there was a creature inside him that would run her to ground if he had to, he needed her so badly.

"No, I want to." Her cheeks stained that pretty shade of pink that stoked the fire in his gut. "It's only that I felt swept away a few minutes ago. Now the mood is a little…" She wrinkled her nose. "Logistical. I'm being silly."

The doors opened, and she stepped out, looking to him to show her the way.

Her befuddling honesty and that phrase *always wondered how these things were handled* made him realize she didn't have the experience he did. It provoked a sort of endeared protectiveness in him. As he brought her to the door of his penthouse, he felt almost as though he was initiating a virgin. He wanted to take care with her and meet all her expectations. These sorts of interludes ought to be nothing but pleasure with no reason for regret. He wanted to give her that.

He wanted to give her the best sex she'd ever had so he would remain in her thoughts forever.

And where the hell had *that* come from?

"Do you want a drink?" He let her in and closed the door, sealing them into a lounge lit only by a table lamp. He threw off his jacket, trying to cool his blood. *Patience*.

"No, thanks." She was clicking the clasp on her purse again.

"I don't do this as often you might think, you know." Not anymore at least. "It suits me to let people think I'm a slut, but I'm actually quite picky."

"Which sounds a little like you're trying to make me feel special. I'll chose to believe you." She set her handbag on a side table and wandered past the sofa to the glass doors that led onto the terrace. Outside, recessed lighting cast pools of gold from beneath the hedges that surrounded the patio table and chairs.

"You are special." He came up behind her and trailed his fingertips down her bare arms, pleased when he heard her breath catch. He was growing addicted to this chemistry that simmered and fizzed between them. It stoked his own arousal, making him twitch and thicken behind his fly. "Do you always react like this?"

"Ha. No." She hugged herself, rubbing the bumps that had risen on her arms. In the faint reflection on the glass, her gaze sought his. "Do you?" Her voice held challenge. Cynicism.

Her question plucked at one of the razor-thin piano wires he used to protect himself. He did not react like this to every woman he met, but he wasn't about to admit it.

"If you want to talk because you're nervous, that's okay." He trailed his fingers down her arms again, making her body twitch in a shudder of sensuality. "But I'd rather you let me sweep you away."

"I am nervous," she admitted breathlessly, voice thinning to a whisper. "But I do want that." She started to turn into his arms.

He stopped her.

"Stay like this," he persuaded, hearing his voice drop into his chest with anticipation.

He drew a line from one side of her neck to the other, scooping her hair onto the front of her shoulder, exposing the bow that secured the haltered front of her gown. He pressed a kiss to her nape.

Such a tiny thing, but it made her shoulders flex. This power he had over her would be heady if there wasn't such an answering ring of need that crashed like a gong inside him. Sexual aggression had its place, but this wasn't it. He kept a tight leash on his inner caveman and nuzzled into the fragrance of almonds and peaches that clung in her hair.

"Can I untie this?" he asked against the strings that dangled against the top of her spine.

"Yes." The word was a rush of breath.

Slowly, slowly, he drew the tail free, watching her shoulder blades pull together as the loops released. He kissed her nape and the tip of her shoulder and scraped his teeth against the tendons at the base of her neck, then bent lower to suck the skin on the fleshy part of her upper arm.

A shiver and a helpless sound was his reward.

As the front of her gown fell forward, exposing her chest in a translucent reflection of pale gold and shadowed nipples, she brought her arms up to shield herself.

He slid his hands around to cup her breasts for her, very aware of the way she drew in a ragged breath at his possessive action. He involuntarily groaned with possessive pleasure as the weight of the warm swells filled his palms.

"Put your hands on the glass." His voice was barely working, coming out graveled by the carnal hunger that was gathering inside him.

The position forced her to lean forward slightly, pushing her ass into his fly and settling her breasts more fully into his hands. He could feel her excitement in the way her breaths trembled, and knowing he was causing it sent electric signals of need straight into his groin.

He stepped even closer, covering her as he continued to kiss her nape and slowly massage the firm globes that filled his hands. He played with her nipples until they were so taut his mouth watered with longing to suck on them. Hard.

She made a noise that sounded like pain.

"Too rough?" He stilled his touch.

"No. It's—I can't…"

"It feels good?" He smiled against her hairline, blowing softly behind her ear as he returned to lightly pinching and toying with her nipples.

"Yes." She hung her head as though tortured beyond her bearing. She shifted restlessly, arching her breasts into his hands while pressing her ass deeper into his crotch, rocking with invitation.

Exquisite.

"Are you feeling needy, angel? Do you want my hands under your skirt? Here?" He released one breast to slide his palm down her stomach, then pressed the fall of silk deep into the hot valley between her thighs. When he flexed his grip against her mound, the noise she made was incredibly erotic, making his skin feel too tight to contain him.

"I like my hand here, too," he assured her in a graveled voice, squeezing in gentle but firm rhythm, enjoying the kinky sensation of trapping her in a vise of pleasure so she shook and wriggled for escape but had nowhere to go.

He nudged her feet open so he could step between them and pressed forward, giving her a firm seat for the grind of her ass against his aching erection while he tongued her earlobe. The sexy noises that emerged from her throat and the rock of her loins against his throbbing sex were an erotic purgatory he could have lived in forever.

"Harder," she moaned, dropping her hand to cover his.

"Keep your hands on the glass, Fliss. Or I'll stop." That was a lie. There was no possible way he wanted to stop. He wanted to fondle her until she broke, but he needed to stay in control. If she started running things, this would be over in a short minute.

He nearly lost it anyway when she dutifully set her hand back on the glass and he glimpsed the way she bit her lips in contrition. Damn, he wanted to kiss that mouth of hers.

But her obedience had granted him permission to continue having his way with her.

With a growled noise of approval, he straightened enough to gather her skirt with both hands until he could burrow beneath the silk to thighs that trembled at his first touch. He stroked all over the warm skin, everywhere that he could reach, from thighs to buttocks to lower back, then forward to her stomach and back down to her thighs.

Her ass wore a V-shaped slash of silver lace held up by three narrow bands of midnight blue strung across her hips. The delicate lace trapped his hand when he slid his touch inside the front. Her plump mound was like holding heaven. She moaned and stepped her feet farther apart, pressing into his touch, all slick and hungry and helpless to her own desires. When she rocked against his fingers, coating them in her essence, he felt omnipotent.

"I want you like this," he said in a guttural voice he barely recognized. "I want to be inside you right here. Like this."

He wanted a thousand other things, too. He wanted his mouth here where his fingers were making her whimper. He wanted her tongue in his mouth and her naked body riding his. He wanted their sweaty bodies contorting into every lewd act he could think of, but right now, he *needed* to be inside her.

Miraculously, she dipped her lower back and lifted her hips with invitation.

"Yes. I want that, too."

Felicity had thought she was waiting for love. For romance. For commitment and a sense of a future with a man. She didn't look down on women who engaged in casual sex, but she had never imagined it was for her. Until now.

Until this man made her feel that walking away without seeing where this could go would be cheating herself in some way. Even in the elevator, as she'd recognized how effortlessly he made clear this was a one-night stand, she had sensed that if she didn't seize this chance to be with him, even for a few hours, she would regret it.

And here she was, regretting nothing, despite behaving in a way that was so flagrant it bordered on debauchery. She was letting him touch her in very intimate ways. He was commanding her to keep her hands on the glass, and she did it because she needed to have sex with him or she would die. Literally *die*. That was how it felt.

When he removed his hand from her tanga, she moaned in loss. But she could feel the brush of his knuckles against her backside as he released himself from his fly.

The hot weight of his erection sat against the lace that descended into the crease of her buttocks. In the glass, she saw him bite the edge of a small square packet.

"I like your underwear," he told her as he covered himself with the condom. "You'll have to bill me for the replacement."

Before she processed what he meant, the thin cords at her hips snapped and they fell away.

"Oh." The sad sob in her throat turned into a more carnal *"Oh"* as he swept his touch all over the flesh he'd bared, reigniting the fires of need inside her.

Then he was guiding the thick crown of his erection to explore those same slick, eager places, seeking her entrance. Prodding.

She bit her lip, tensing. She'd only done this once before, literally once. Would it hurt the same way?

The pressure increased, hinting at discomfort, but she was so wet and he was so gradual, giving light pulses of his hips as he rolled his fingertip around the swollen knot of her clit. He teased her into relaxing and accepting the unfamiliar intrusion.

At the last moment, she instinctually arched, and that was it. He slid all the way in so his hips were flush against her buttocks. The fabric of his trousers was an abrasion against the backs of her thighs. His steely shape stretched and filled her so she quivered at the thoroughness of his possession.

His hands clasped her hips, holding her steady. His breath hissed, then he leaned over her and his teeth opened against her nape, threatening to bite before he turned it into a hot, wet suckle that had her toes curling in her shoes.

She didn't know how to make sense of all these sensations. The combination of hot arousal and erotic titillation and the wildness of the whole experience was overwhelming, quelling her ability to think. She simply *was*.

He started to move, and the magnitude of the experience exploded.

Waves of pleasure rolled up and down her body with the slide of his hand across her naked torso. The retreat and return of his lovemaking was carnal and raw and so delicious she couldn't help making animalistic noises of pleasure. She was an animal. She'd been caught in the forest by a potential mate, and that was what they were doing. Mating. It was earthy and primal and pure.

"Can you come like this?" he asked against her ear. "Or do you need…" His long fingers swept to the front of her thighs again. He caressed where he was moving with slow, deliberate power, then higher, plucking at her swollen clit.

A storm gathered within her. She couldn't speak because all the energy in the universe had shrunk to a fine point inside her. All that existed was the astounding pleasure coiling in her loins, gathering.

In rough desperation, she pushed herself backward into his thrusts, increasing the impact of his hips.

He grunted in surprise. One hand shifted to bite into her waist, and the speed of his thrusts increased. His hips slapped her buttocks, and the nucleus of need inside her detonated, expanding outward like a supernova.

She cried out with the strength of her climax, but his shout was louder. He pounded into her, engulfing her in a fire that should have incinerated her but only licked and burned and melded her so indelibly with him, she didn't imagine how they could ever be separated.

Saint left later than he should have and had to sleep on the flight rather than using the time to prepare his presentation as he'd originally planned. That was his first misstep.

He hadn't meant to crash on impact, but the dubious thrill of creating slides of market analysis tables was no match for his lack of sleep and abundance of energetic sex.

What the hell had even happened to him? He'd been wrung dry in those first moments in the living room. He'd been emptied of thought and strength and purpose by an orgasm that had bordered on pain it had been so powerful.

He should have soothed them both with a cuddle on the couch and a glass of wine. He'd felt inordinately tender, given how she'd been trembling, but when he'd withdrawn and turned her, their lazy kisses had caught fire again as quickly as their first.

His dumb stick had hardened, and his hunger for her had sharpened to acute. When he'd drawn back, both of them gasping for air, he'd been half barbarian, ordering her gruffly, *Get into my bed. I want to do that again.*

She had said exactly what she'd been saying to him all night. *Yes.*

What a drug. What a night. His orgasms had gotten better and better every time. He couldn't even count how many she'd had. He would've been delivering another several right now if he'd stayed, which he'd been very tempted to do.

That was why he'd made himself leave—while she'd been sound asleep. Otherwise, he suspected he wouldn't have been able to. But this meeting with his father and the rest of the board was too important. The fact that he'd considered risking their ire by rescheduling so he could stay and make love with Fliss had been enough of a caution light that he'd decided it was better to put space between him and the spell she'd cast over him.

Even so, he was still reliving that incredible sex when he arrived in New York and jumped into the shower of the hospitality suite below his office. He was *recovering*, he noted ruefully, and turned the tap of the shower to cold, then downed a hot coffee while he dressed in a clean shirt and suit.

Saint ought to have been mentally preparing for what would be a typically abrasive encounter with his father, but his libido was pacing restlessly inside him, griping, *When can I see her again?*

Never, if he was a jerk about it and failed to express his appreciation for their very exceptional night.

It wasn't like him to be so punch-drunk from any woman, let alone one he'd just met. Hell, he still barely knew her. Most of their conversation later in the night had revolved around, *Does this feel good?*

"Sir?" His assistant, Willow, poked their head in. They were nonbinary, usually wearing a suit and tie for work while keeping their long red hair in a tidy bun. Occasionally they wore eyeshadow behind the ever-changing frames of their glasses, and they changed their colorful shades of nail polish almost daily. "The board is assembled and ready for you."

"One minute." He handed Willow the notes he'd scribbled as he'd made his way from the jet to the helipad on top of this tower.

He should have been first to the meeting and was already ten minutes late, but he took out his phone and found the number for Smythe's in his contacts.

"Mr. Montgomery." The smooth, feminine voice of Ms. Smythe greeted him in her cool boarding-school accent. "How may I serve you today? I have an opening in an hour."

"I'm in New York," he replied. "But I'd like to purchase some earrings. Something like you showed me last time." He'd intended to give Julie a pair to wear to the gala, but Fliss deserved something he picked out especially for her. "Something with blue in them." The shade of her gown was imprinted in his memory forever.

"Contemporary? Let me text you a few photos. One moment."

Smythe's was a mystery—both shop and owner—but Saint had been warned that prying would result in his no longer receiving invitations to shop there, which would be a pity. He'd dealt with many high-end jewelry merchants throughout his adult life, and Ms. Smythe of Knightsbridge was the best. She was professional and discreet. Her gemstones were ethically sourced and always of the highest quality, the settings one of a kind. Saint occasionally bought investment pieces but more often purchased a parting gift when a liaison was wrapping up.

Today he was looking for more of a welcome gift.

His phone pinged. He flicked through the photos. One

showed a chandelier of blue sapphires in yellow gold; another was a platinum cuff with alternate rows of diamonds and sapphires.

"The ones with the marquis diamonds," he told Ms. Smythe. The earrings were the size of a silver dollar. The leaf-shaped white diamonds formed a laurel wreath around an eye-catching twist of round-cut blue sapphires. They radiated elegance and graceful artistry but maintained a playful quality that he thought suited Fliss.

"A lovely choice. Are these for delivery, or shall I hold them for you?"

"Delivery. Her name is Fliss." His inner beast had been too focused on sex to ask for her number before she'd fallen asleep. "She's a fashion designer, but you'll have to do some legwork for me."

Saint had peeked into her purse on his way out the door. He'd found a twenty-pound note, her smartphone, which had been locked, a pair of physical door keys—who even used those anymore?—an invitation to the gala, an Oyster card and a lip gloss. Not even a driver's license or a debit card to give him her full name.

The gala invitation had had Delia Chevron's name on it, which made sense. A model would have friends in fashion. He'd written his number on the card, then slipped away.

"Check the hotel," he said to Ms. Smythe, mentioning the one he always used when visiting London. "If she's still in the room, you can deliver to her there." He had meant to take care of this while he'd been flying to ensure he wouldn't miss her, but so much for that. She'd worn him out, and he'd needed his beauty sleep. "If she's already gone, contact Delia Chevron. They were supposed to attend last night's art gala together, so she'll know how to reach her."

Actually, Fliss had said she had known her date wouldn't be there. Saint spared a moment to ponder that. He'd been so taken with her, he'd glossed over how cagey she'd been about her reason for attending and leaving before it had really started.

"I'd love an excuse to connect with Ms. Chevron." Ms. Smythe's warm voice redirected his thoughts back to the business at hand. "I'll be in touch once your gift has been delivered."

"Thank you." He ended the call and strode down the hall to begin the presentation he would have to make up on the fly.

He wasn't worried. He had spent the last year and a half taking a new approach to military-grade encryption software, personally establishing proof of concept before writing the code for the prototype. This was his baby, and he knew it inside and out.

His father preferred to spearhead product innovation. That would be the stumbling block. Theodore Montgomery had an ego to match the fortune and tech empire he'd built. His control of Grayscale was of the tight, iron-fist variety. In his mind, he was the only genius in the family. His son was far more suited to what Fliss had called "glad-handing."

Saint knew this software would be his contribution to the legacy of his name, though. It would allow him to step out from under his father's shadow and be seen as an innovator in his own right. A leader of the next generation in the technological revolution.

The project was ready for the next stage of development.

He needed a team of top-tier programmers to build it out, improve the interface, test it, refine it, then take it to market. That required a huge investment of time, money and other resources. Since it would also become Grayscale's next flagship product, he needed the board on board.

"Good morning," he said as he entered the room filled with middle-aged suits and skirts. On the screen at one end of the room were another half dozen faces, all pinched with expressions of disapproval. His father looked at his watch.

Willow, first-class executive assistant with a minor in miracle making, had translated Saint's chicken scratch into slides that appeared with the click of a button.

Saint dove straight into his business case, emphasizing the value and benefits this software would have for Grayscale, including its appeal to both high-level institutions and small-business users.

"We already offer encryption software," someone said.

"This one is better." It was sacrilege to claim anything his father had designed needed improvement, but it did. "This will become the preferred solution," Saint promised.

The protests kept coming, though, making Saint look to his father, starting to suspect that Ted had poisoned the well before Saint had entered the room.

"You're asking for a lot of money to make a copycat product."

"Are you really prepared to take on a project this complex and carry it across the line? It could take years."

"There's a difference between charm and leadership, Saint."

"Don't hold back," Saint drawled to hide his irritation. "Tell me what you really think of me."

"We think it's half-baked, son," Ted Montgomery said. "Did you not pick up on that?"

"Of course it's half-baked. That's why I'm here. To get an oven," he shot back.

"It feels premature," the CFO said soothingly while looking around to collect nods of agreement.

"No problem." Holding his father's stare, Saint said, "I'll start my own company and develop it myself." It was the contingency plan he had hoped not to need. It would be far more convenient to develop this under the Grayscale umbrella. It would integrate better, and he didn't want it to belong to anyone else when he eventually inherited Grayscale.

"With my money? You're exactly like your mother," his father accused in his scoffing way, right there in front of the assembled board. "You think you can help yourself to what's behind door number three and use it for whatever pissant idea arrives in your head."

"Actually, Dad, I'm exactly like you." Saint took his ire and offense and any other emotion he was currently experiencing and condensed it inside himself. He *became* his father, sharp and hard and clear as a diamond. Able to cut through anything. "This is a business decision. I'm about to revolutionize the sector. If you're so shortsighted that you want to cut me off financially, I'll pick up the phone and ask one of our competitors to develop this with me. Frankly, I'd prefer to focus on this without the distraction of running Grayscale."

Which he did run, whether his father wanted to acknowledge that or not.

Ted wore the title of president and had the final say on top-level decisions, but his social skills were abysmal. Saint

spent half his life on a plane. Under the guise of schmooz-
ing, he kept an eye on the executives in their global of-
fices, ironing out wrinkles before they became problems.
He resolved sticky issues around politics and international
regulations and carried the emotional burden of those who
were frustrated by his father's closed-minded leadership
so his father wasn't bothered by power struggles and other
conflicts.

"I'm well aware you regard this company as a distraction," Ted said with heavy sarcasm, waving toward the
screen mounted on the wall. It was back to showing the
remote board members, but Saint got the message that his
name and face were appearing on screens for all the wrong
reasons, thanks to Julie. "You couldn't even stay for dinner last night because you were chasing a new skirt. Clean
up your act, son. Show me you're serious about taking the
reins, and maybe I could think about retiring. Then you
can pour my money into whatever hairbrained scheme you
like."

Saint snorted. "You're never going to retire."

The man was seventy and came into the office daily so
he could bark orders and continue to feel important. The
power he'd amassed here was the only thing that gave him
anything close to a sense of satisfaction with his life.

Saint turned his attention to the room at large.

"Just so we're clear, this prototype was built on my own
time, on my own equipment, by me. It's mine," he said.
"There are people intrigued enough by what I create to want
to steal it. They know what I did with the early AI configu-
rations, and they want to know what I'm up to next." That
was why Julie had been nudged by her debtors to copy his

files. "My work has value. Maybe not to you, but I won't let that slow me down."

He gathered up his laptop and walked out.

"Saint." One of his allies on the board caught him outside the door. "Don't do anything rash. Give me some time to change some minds. There are a lot of people on your side." He nodded toward the boardroom.

"Oh, really," Saint snorted.

"Especially when it comes to your eventual rise to the throne. But they can't get behind you unless they know you're ready. Maybe take your father's advice? Showing up late today only gave everyone a chance to gossip about you. Maybe if they didn't have anything to gossip about…"

Saint hated to back down or put off his goals, but he also knew his father wasn't stupid. Ted might have flexed his muscles for their audience, but when it came to dollars and sense, he would do what was best for Grayscale.

So would Saint, and honestly, the publicity he'd generated with Julie wasn't great for Grayscale.

"Point taken," he muttered and detoured to the head of their PR department on his way back to his office.

"Xanthe," he greeted as he entered her office.

She was a chic single mother of two who always appeared to be fully in control. Saint suspected she had her days, same as everyone, but the fact that no one ever saw her in a state of stress was a testament to her skill at manipulating optics.

"Saint." She wore her black hair in a neat bun and had her pointed collar turned up around her chin. "You were on my calendar to see today." She left her desk to join him where he was making himself at home on her sofa.

"Because of Julie? I just took a whipping over that, thanks. No one appreciates the free publicity I generate to keep Grayscale a household name."

"Some people are so ungrateful, aren't they?" she mused. "Perhaps if you hadn't poured gasoline on her 'woman scorned' routine by moving on so quickly?"

Fliss? "It was a few photos at the curb. They'll turn anything into a story, won't they?"

"Who is she?" Xanthe asked.

He started to say *No one*, but that didn't feel right. He skipped past answering and said, "I've been informed that my image needs work. What do you suggest?"

"Honestly? Marriage. To someone appropriate," she added quickly. "Conservative. A good family. Well-known, but not famous. Not *in*famous."

"Not interested," Saint said flatly. He'd had a front-row seat on the train wreck that was his parents' marriage. It should have been dissolved decades ago. As far as he was concerned, marriage was nothing less than a cage fight to the death.

"An engagement, then," Xanthe said with her signature ability to pivot. "Temporary. It doesn't have to be real, but it would convey that you're settling down."

Fliss leapt to mind, but he didn't want to bring her into a fake engagement while they had a real affair. Too messy. And if he engaged himself to someone else, he couldn't see her.

"No."

"All right. Final offer." Xanthe used a tone of exaggerated patience and leaned back while crossing her legs. "Celibacy. And I'll circulate rumors that you're *looking* for a wife. That signals you're maturing and developing a sense of responsibility."

"I *have* a sense of responsibility. That's why I'm here. But sure. Run with that." He flicked his hand.

"Did you hear the part about living like a monk? It won't work if you continue having affairs."

"I know."

"Do you?"

He liked Xanthe, he really did, but she was annoying as hell in how well she saw through him.

"Look," he said with the same exaggerated patience she was using. "There is an image that served me well for a long time but no longer does. That's why I'm here. *I* have changed, even if the narrative hasn't."

"I know you don't have nearly as many affairs as you're reported to have," she acknowledged smoothly. "I also know that when I say 'no women,' you hear 'except that one you really want to have an affair with.' I mean none, Saint."

He looked away, dismayed. He did want an affair with one particular woman. She was all the way across the Atlantic, though. And he hadn't made any promises to her. He could absolutely leave her with the earrings and never contact her again.

"This is important to me," he stated decisively. "I need the board to know I'm all grown up and can be trusted with the keys to the car."

"I'll start the whispers today."

"Thank you." He nodded and rose.

"You're going to call her, aren't you?" Xanthe said, staying seated while watching him knowingly.

"We'll keep it under the radar," he promised. He ignored the *tsk* he heard as he left.

He was far more disturbed by Ms. Smythe's report when he got back to his office.

Delia Chevron didn't know any designers named Fliss.

CHAPTER FOUR

"You can't steal from clients, Felicity." Her supervisor, Luz, was dark red beneath her normally light brown complexion.

"I didn't steal," Fliss argued weakly. "It was in the bin."

But it had been wrong to take the invitation. She had known it was wrong when she'd taken it out of the bin. And when she'd stuck it in her handbag. She had been dead wrong to put it in her clutch and carry that wretched card to the art gallery.

She wanted to sink through the floor with humiliation and guilt that she'd ever even noticed the darned thing.

"You've cost me a good client." Luz's voice rang with anger. "You know I can't keep you on."

"I know," Fliss mumbled, feeling sick.

For three days, she had thought she had gotten away with her futile attempt to advance herself. Photos of her with Saint had turned up online, but none had shown her face very well, so no one had recognized her.

Then, this morning, she'd been told to report here to Luz before starting her shift at a luxury flat in Chelsea. Fliss had known immediately that her dark deed had come to light. Her stomach had begun to churn.

"Did you really have *sex* with Saint Montgomery?" Luz hissed.

"What?" That knocked Fliss back in her chair. "Why do you think that?"

"Because he's *Saint Montgomery*. You went to his hotel with him, then he tried to send you earrings through Delia Chevron. You left them in his room, I presume?" Luz elevated her brows with disdain.

"What? *No*." She touched her earlobe, which was naked, but she had definitely come home with the hoops she'd worn to the gala. She was deeply confused. "I don't know anything about any earrings. That doesn't make sense."

"Which is what Delia said. She pieced together that someone had attended the gala with an invitation addressed to her and had her team investigate how you came by it."

"I didn't pretend to be her," Fliss rushed to assert. She had only implied she was Delia's plus-one, then had been shuffled off to the side to wait for her. She didn't explain that Saint was the one who had actually brought her into the gallery. "He hasn't called *you*, has he? Did you give him my number?"

Luz glared outrage at her.

"I'm not saying you should," Fliss mumbled. Where was astral traveling when you really needed it? She would give anything not to be inhabiting her body in this profoundly mortifying moment.

"I'm really disappointed in you, Felicity. I thought you were someone I could count on. Your final pay will go into your account overnight. I cannot give you a reference, but I wish you well in future." Luz straightened a stack of papers that didn't need straightening, signaling this discussion was over.

"I'm genuinely sorry, Luz." Fliss rose. She was tongue-tied, unable to find anything more to say that wasn't full out groveling.

Her only hope was that this incident wouldn't follow her around like a bad smell, the way those awful rumors started by her old boyfriend had.

She went home and, since her workday had barely started, pulled up her CV on her ancient laptop. She was immediately disheartened. Scrubbing toilets was her top skill these days, but without a reference she wasn't even fit for that. The fashion design route was even further out of reach.

She couldn't waste time on berating herself, though. There would be ample time for that later. For now, she needed to make rent.

Perhaps she *should* go back to school. It was months until September, though.

Fliss looked around her room with its chipped sill and saggy bed and toilet down the hall. It wasn't much, but it had enough space for her sewing machine and table, her form and a tall, cardboard wardrobe where she stored her finished creations.

She could sell those, she supposed, but that would be counterproductive to her aspirations. Plus, experience had taught her that she would be lucky to earn back the cost of the fabric, especially when she was in a hurry to sell. She rarely got enough to cover her many hours of labor.

As for the gown, she could barely look at it.

She was both appalled and elated when she thought about

her night with Saint. Nearly everything about it had been perfect, from the way he'd swept her into the glamor of the gala, then taken her for such a fancy dinner. She'd felt like Cinderella. Maybe she hadn't been fully on his level socially and financially, but she hadn't felt as far away as this life put her.

And the sex. If that was what she'd been missing all this time, she had a newfound contempt for her old boyfriend for making her think sex was something you worked up the courage to offer someone. With Saint, there'd been surprisingly little awkwardness. She had reveled in sharing herself with him. He'd been equally generous with his body and kisses and skill.

When she'd awakened in that wide bed on those luxurious sheets, she'd been pleasantly sore all over, feeling as though she'd hiked to a challenging peak and was brimming with accomplishment. As though she'd won the lottery and could live her life on her own terms from now on.

The first knock of reality had arrived when she had discovered she was alone.

Saint had warned her that he'd had an early flight, so she had tried not to let his disappearance bother her, but it had felt a bit tawdry that he'd slipped away without saying goodbye. She'd splurged on a car share rather than a walk of shame on the tube. She had been home and emptying her clutch before she'd found the number he'd scrawled with *Call me* on the back of the invitation that bore Delia Chevron's name.

Chagrin had wormed into her at that point, boring holes in her midsection. Fliss hadn't lied to him about who she was. She hadn't dropped Delia's name to impress him, but his knowing that she'd possessed that card made her reluctant to text the number he'd given her. If she were a student at this point, she might have felt more confident in connecting with him again, but she was now an unemployed housekeeper and she didn't have a good way to explain that card.

She peered into the nightstand drawer where she had left it, keeping his note like a war bride holding on to a love letter. Should she text and ask What is this about earrings?

Oh, God. He wasn't trying to *pay* her, was he?

That felt tawdry. Sex work was fine for people who chose it, but she was ultrasensitive to how she was perceived sexually, especially when it was a wrong impression. Had he thought that was what her motive had been in going to that gala? Did he think she'd been trolling for a sugar daddy?

Fliss buried her face in her hands, ready to do anything to go back in time and not take that card!

Which would mean she wouldn't have the memory of those few magical hours with him.

No. She dropped her hands from her face. Much as she regretted how things had turned out at work, she didn't regret that night. Saint had helped her discover a passion she hadn't known she could feel. It had been a wonderful experience and now it was over and that left her wistful, but fine. She would suffer the consequence of her impulsive theft of that card, find another job and never see him again. Her boring little life would go on.

She believed that right up until her phone rang the next day. It was a reporter for one of the tabloids.

"Are you the Felicity Corning who was with Saint Montgomery last weekend?"

* * *

"People keep asking me for a statement. This is my statement," Delia Chevron said on her social media reel.

Saint took the phone from Willow to watch the slender brunette with a wide mouth and eyelids that sat at a bored half-mast.

"I've never met Saint Montgomery or Felicity Corning. She was working for a housekeeping agency and took an invitation from my home that she used to get into the gala. The next day, Mr. Montgomery tried to send earrings to her, through me. This alerted me to the theft. My security team recommended I end my contract with the agency, so I have. That's all I know. Don't ask me for dirt on any of them. I don't have any."

"I do." Julie had spliced Delia's statement into the front of her own so the video cut to her in the back of a car. She wore a ponytail and yoga clothes to give the impression this was an impromptu reaction, but she wore full make-up and he would bet his encryption software that she was getting paid to wear that brand.

"This is how he operates," Julie told the viewer. "He'll sleep with anyone, even a light-fingered housekeeper. And the earrings? Judging from where they were purchased, they're worth at least two hundred thousand pounds. In fact, they were probably purchased for *me*. I was meant to attend that gala with him. He told me he'd have something pretty for me to wear, then he dumped me. For *her*. Although I wouldn't doubt he was trying to get Delia's attention. Watch out, girlfriend. That man is a playa…"

Saint swore and clicked off the phone, handing it back to Willow.

"I'm going to have to take legal action against her, aren't I?" he muttered.

"Who?"

"What do you mean 'who'? The woman destroying my reputation," Saint snapped.

Willow drew a breath and held it, as though still at a loss.

He swore again. "The woman who is *intentionally* destroying my reputation for the paycheck she's earning off her viral clicks." Although all of these women were contributing to this debacle in their own special way. He couldn't blame Willow for not being sure which one was causing him the most irritation. "Did you send the apology to Delia?"

"With a gift basket and an offer to cover her PR costs."

"Good. And Ms. Smythe?"

"Has the earrings. You're not out of pocket. She has also received a gift basket and some tickets for an opening in the West End as compensation for her trouble. I had the sense that future calls from you might go to voicemail."

No doubt. Saint scratched his eyebrow. How had one night turned into this?

"What about Fliss? Any word from her?" He braced himself as he picked up his phone to look for a text, not sure what kind of reaction he expected from her. Something that monetized her own notoriety? Blame for the attention that had fallen onto her? An apology for not being completely honest with him?

Nothing. Not even a redirection for delivery of the earrings.

"Her socials have been switched to private," Willow said.

"She hasn't returned to the house in London. Her house-mates are quoted as not knowing where she went."

Fliss had been photographed leaving her home five days ago, when gossip from her coworkers had leaked to the press. She'd since found a good place to hide because she wasn't turning up online. That was both a relief and a frustration for Saint.

He didn't love that she'd hidden so much about who she really was, but she hadn't been outright dishonest, either.

Are we prevaricating?

I'm out of my league.

He was dismayed to hear she'd stolen from a client's home. It was too much like Julie's laptop snooping for his comfort. It made him wonder if Fliss was hiding from paparazzi while she negotiated the best way to capitalize on her night with him—the way Julie had.

"I did find some background on her that was...concerning," Willow continued.

"I've seen what the trolls are saying," Saint grumbled.

"They claim to be childhood friends."

"Friends don't say things like that about friends." And who cared if she'd had an active sex life? So had he.

No, those rumors bothered him for a different reason. They didn't fit with the inexperience she'd expressed.

I've always wondered how these things were handled.

If she was as practiced as those rumors suggested, he would have expected less bashfulness, more assertiveness. She'd been enthusiastic as hell while they'd been making love, which was the part that really mattered, but maybe playing an ingenue was her kink?

Role-play was fine, too, but he hated feeling gullible.

He didn't want to believe he'd fallen for an act when he'd been fully involved and as real as he could be for those few hours.

He didn't want to question his own acuity when his father and the board were already doing that for him.

Saint's phone rang. He glanced to see that it was his father and muttered another curse under his breath.

"I'm talking to the lawyers right now," he said in lieu of a greeting, then rolled his wrist at Willow to get on it. He wouldn't out Julie for her gambling addiction, but… "I'll have them threaten a defamation suit if she doesn't cease and desist."

Ted ignored that. "Your mother is asking why you have two hundred thousand pounds for a prostitute's earrings—"

"She is *not*—"

"But I won't bankroll another thoroughbred. Make that go away." His father ended the call.

"Fuuuun…" Saint groaned at the ceiling, crushing his phone in his grip. He was tempted to throw it against the wall.

"Tell Legal to inform Julie that I *will* pursue industrial espionage charges if she doesn't keep my name out of her mouth," he told Willow. He reached for the extra-strength acetaminophen in his desk drawer and swallowed two before he tapped his mother's number. "Interrupt me in ten minutes with a life-or-death emergency."

"Mrs. Bhamra? I'm back," Fliss called over the Bollywood musical playing on the senior's television.

She was later than usual, having picked up a few things on her way home and detoured to view a bedsit. She loved being here. It was almost like being home with Granny, but it had been more than two weeks. She didn't want to overstay her welcome.

Mrs. Bhamra had become Granny's best friend back when the pair had been young widows raising their children on their wages from the lace factory. They had lost their jobs at the same time when the factory had closed but had continued to bolster each other through the rest of life's ups and downs—job changes and weddings and grandchildren, Granny's loss of her son and Mrs. Bhamra's battle with breast cancer.

The pair had had a standing date twice a month where they drank tea and exchanged gossip, romance novels and knitting patterns. Mrs. Bhamra had teased Granny about her belief in psychics, and Granny had complained that Mrs. Bhamra's curry was too spicy. Otherwise, they'd been stamped from the same mold, or so Granny had always said.

As they'd both aged, Fliss had moved back into Granny's modest flat while Mrs. Bhamra had moved to the upscale Mapperley Park, where her son had converted a coach house into a sunny bungalow. It was one floor so she didn't have to climb stairs and had a guest bedroom that her sister used when she visited from Canada. The front window looked onto the landscaped garden where a bridge crossed a pond before its path continued to the steps of the mansion that was the main house.

When Fliss had turned up in the *Daily Mail* next to Saint Montgomery, Mrs. Bhamra had called to ask if the photograph was really her. Since Fliss had been on the verge of hysteria, realizing she was in far worse trouble than simply losing her job, she'd come as clean as she would have to Granny.

Mrs. Bhamra had offered her guest room, much to the chagrin of her son, Ujjal. He wasn't 100 percent thrilled to have Fliss here. He knew as well as she did that the paps would figure out where she was eventually, especially now that she was leaving the house to go to work.

The job was janitorial work for an assisted living facility, thanks to Ujjal making a call, but it was a foot in the door. They were desperate for care aids, too. Fliss could attain her certificate with only a few courses, and that would improve her pay. She was actively looking for her own place, planning to be on her own again very soon.

Provided, of course, that this persistent tummy bug was actually a tummy bug and not what she was starting to suspect it was.

"You worked late today," Mrs. Bhamra said as she muted the television.

"I stopped to buy a few things for dinner." Fliss shrugged out of the baggie hoodie she wore whenever she went out, adding sunglasses like every poorly disguised criminal on the run in every heist movie. "Let me change and wash up, then I'll get started."

"You don't have to cook for me," Mrs. Bhamra protested. She often ate at the house with her family or her daughter-in-law brought a plate if it was a gloomy day and Mrs. Bhamra preferred to stay here.

"I want to." Fliss might've been borderline destitute, but she drew the line at imposing on the elderly woman's family. She ate groceries she bought, sharing as often as she could but mostly subsisting on peanut butter toast.

If her suspicions were correct, she needed to start eating more vegetables and probably get some special vitamins.

"Do you know I've been thinking of your grandmother all day?" Mrs. Bhamra mused.

"Oh?" Fliss paused in starting toward her room. "I did a reading this morning. I must have conjured her, and she decided to stay and watch your shows with you."

"Pfft." Mrs. Bhamra waved that away with amusement. "I did watch a very nice travel program that she would have enjoyed. The host was some fool traveling around the world. He started at the Eiffel Tower, forgot his sunscreen in Australia, got himself stung by a scorpion in America. Did you know they had those there?"

"Scorpions? No." Fliss pushed a smile onto her lips, but her heart began thudding so hard she grew lightheaded.

The three cards she'd pulled this morning had all been from the Major Arcana—the Sun, the Tower, and the Fool. They were such a powerful combination, she'd barely functioned all day, trying to work out what they meant.

As if the universe was trying to be subtle. The Fool represented blind faith, but it might as well have been a hand mirror. *She* was the fool. The Tower indicated unexpected events. It showed a tower being struck by lightning, throwing two people plummeting to the ground. She was definitely in freefall, but she hadn't meant to cause Saint's downfall along with her own.

Finally, the Sun indicated the beginning of a new life cycle. Given she would have to reinvent herself after losing the life she'd made in London, drawing that particular card made sense. The fact that it showed a naked baby on a horse was just a coincidence. Surely.

"Oh, Granny," she whispered as she slipped into the powder room. "Help me. Please, please, please."

She didn't know what outcome she was praying for as she unpacked the pregnancy test. It seemed ridiculous to even be bothering. She and Saint had used condoms. Yes, they'd had a lot of sex that night, but *they'd used condoms*.

Still, her cycle had always been regular as clockwork. She had nursed denial for five days, desperately trying to believe the stress of hiding from the press was making her late. That lateness was making her feel queasy. She wasn't pregnant.

She knew, though. She knew what she would see.

Positive.

How could such a simple procedure, such a thin pale line, upend her life so completely?

As she sat on the closed lid of the toilet staring at the result, she had to fight the pressure of emotive tears that rose behind her eyes.

She knew she had options. She knew that raising a baby alone was *hard*. Especially when your income was scant and unreliable. At least her grandmother had had a small settlement from the crash that had killed Fliss's parents. That had helped keep the wolves from the door, but that was long gone to Granny's final years of care. Fliss didn't have that sort of cushion. Aside from Mrs. Bhamra, she didn't have anyone who cared about her, and she'd already taken advantage of the elderly woman enough.

There were social services to help, she knew, but even with assistance she was in for a long and difficult struggle. Her dream of becoming a fashion designer was firmly down the loo. Even finding the sort of job that would support her and a baby would be complicated, given this awful black mark of stealing she had on her record. Then there was the notoriety of the baby's father.

In response to all the questions about her, Saint had made a statement that he didn't discuss his private life in the public sphere, but that wasn't stopping the rest of the world from not only pursuing but also capitalizing on her mistake. She'd seen those awful videos from his other lover, disparaging her as a lowly housekeeper and a thief. There were memes all over the internet about her now, too.

My retainer went missing. The housekeeper wore it to the dentist, pretending to be me. Now my celebrity crush is asking for earrings. #RichPeopleProblems

It was excruciating.

I'm being punished, Granny, I really am.

Fliss felt as though she was being punished for ever having dreams in the first place. She shouldn't compound her situation by giving the world more reason to mock her. Bringing a baby into this mess she'd made would be a terrible mistake.

And how would Saint react? Blame her? Maybe he'd accuse her of getting herself pregnant on purpose to come after his money, but she had truly believed she was protected.

He had used condoms.

As the reality of her situation began to take hold, everything in her was folding in on itself. Having this baby would be a huge mistake. A disaster. She could see that clear as day.

But deep inside, she imagined she already felt a physical presence, as though the baby was a living, burning glow. It was the spark of connection to Fliss's parents, whose loss had left her devastated for years. And Granny, who she missed so badly right this minute her eyes began to leak the tears that were brimmed against her lashes.

If she didn't have this baby—for any reason—she would mourn its loss as deeply as she mourned the rest of her family. This baby *was* her family. She wanted a child.

This baby was *hers*. It didn't matter what anyone thought of her or the father—

She caught her breath, blinking to clear the blur from her vision.

That was it! The paparazzi had interviewed some of her old schoolmates who had revived that awful reputation that she was loose. For once, those rumors might actually serve her. She could claim paternity was a gray area.

Could she? White lies had gotten her into this mess, but at least she had a fresh approach to consider as she carefully put the test back into its packaging and crumpled it inside the bag, checking first that there was no receipt with her name on it. She would toss it into a public dumpster at some point, but for the moment her heart was lighter as she looked forward to her new life, one that included the baby she was going to have.

CHAPTER FIVE

SAINT HAD BEEN in London three times since the gala more than three months ago. Each time, he had thought about reaching out to Fliss.

He'd fought the compulsion with difficulty, especially once paparazzi had located her living in Nottingham. She was working in an assisted living facility and picked up casual shifts at a local pub.

Interest in her was finally dying down, though, largely due to the fact that she only ever said "No comment" and shoved her way past anyone trying to pry more out of her.

Saint was grateful for her silence. A strongly worded letter had quieted Julie, and Saint was doing his best to live up to his name for the sake of his project. He arrived early for meetings, bought his mother a filly she wanted and was enjoying celibacy. Not.

The fact was going without sex wasn't that difficult. He'd gone long stretches in his life without anyone warming his sheets. When he was focused on work, as he'd been through much of last year, he became as single-minded and neglectful of others as his father had always been. It was another reason he'd never pursued relationships that lasted longer than a few weeks. He wasn't built for them.

What did make it hard, pun intended, was his memories of Fliss. He regularly woke in the middle of the night, aching and covered in the sweat of arousal, traces of her touch evaporating from his skin.

He'd made great strides in rehabilitating his reputation, though. Xanthe's constructed gossip about his "eye on the future" and readiness "to find his life partner" had gone a long way with the board. He'd been fielding requests for more information from them for weeks. A few had even confided that his success with this project would give them a reason to pressure his father into retirement.

Yesterday, Saint had been invited to attend their regular quarterly meeting in two days. He was certain that meant they were pivoting toward approval.

His father was still holding his cards close to his chest, and Saint had an idea why. This "life partner" narrative had opened a new field of war between his parents. They had begun advancing their preferred candidates for daughter-in-law.

Saint had played this game before. He knew that siding with one would make his life a living hell with the other. It was freaking exhausting.

From the outside, most would assume that aligning with his father was the strategic move. Not only did they share the common interest of the business, but Saint should know which side his bread was buttered on.

Saint refused to be a hostage to his legacy, though. Many, many times he'd stood on the precipice of walking away from his father's dictates and heavy-handed attempts to control him, aware that he would be walking away from his inheritance.

That didn't bother him. He knew his own worth. Yes, his father had paid for his education, but Saint had done the work to achieve top grades and the two degrees he held. He had put in the hours at the office, too, learning the ins and outs of every department and contributing to the company's success from the time he'd begun sweeping floors at eleven.

No matter where he landed, he would never have to start from the bottom.

He hated to draw his mother into his power struggle with his father, though. Unlike Ted, Norma Montgomery had once possessed a heart. It had since been shattered so often by Saint's father that it was a distorted reflection of the woman Saint remembered from childhood, but he felt obliged to protect her from further damage.

Leaving Grayscale would force her to decide whether she wanted to divorce her husband in what would be a very public, destructive battle or lose her son. Ted would have no compunction about demanding she cut ties with Saint if she wanted to maintain the life to which she had grown accustomed—and the horses she loved as much as, probably more than, her son.

Any decision Saint made around walking away from Grayscale would affect Grayscale, too. He didn't want to destroy something that he'd had a hand in building. He didn't want to take his work to a competitor that would attempt to eat what should have been his. He didn't want to see someone else take over his legacy when his father was finally gone, not when it could be his.

No, the most sensible plan was to continue his restraint, earn the trust of his father and the board, and focus on the product he believed in. With recent scrutiny by the government around privacy, his father couldn't deny the value in his new approach. If his father wanted to tie his agreement to an arranged marriage, they would work that out away from the office.

All of which caused the text Saint received to fill him with conflict.

I have to be in London tomorrow. Is there any chance you're here? I need to speak to you, but I don't want anyone to see us together.

She didn't identify herself, but he gave very few people this number.

Seeing Fliss could reignite the publicity and wouldn't be fair to her if she was looking for something longer term. It could undo the progress he'd made where the board was concerned. The smart thing to do was to leave the text on Read. Or simply say no.

But the temptation to see her was mouth-wateringly strong. All he could think about was the feel of her hand tucked into his arm as they had walked into the hotel. Of her secretive smile, as though she knew things he didn't. Of the way she felt when she shuddered with orgasm, triggering his own.

He deserved answers around why she'd misrepresented herself, didn't he?

That was a rationalization. *We all trick ourselves*, she'd said, and he'd come to realize how very insightful she was.

He looked to the calendar. He was due down the hall here at the New York office less than forty-eight hours from now, but he had turned around a flight to London in less before.

He had Willow rearrange his lesser appointments and file a flight plan, then texted her.

A card will be waiting under the name Norma at the concierge. Come to my hotel room at four p.m.

Time crawled, but after a heavy morning of dull meetings, he was in his hotel room, nursing a scotch while he waited. He was half expecting some enterprising reporter would turn up, but when the knock sounded and the mechanism released, Fliss entered.

He wasn't sure what he had expected, but it wasn't her in a pink plaid skirt suit, black knee-high boots and a beret. It was cute as hell and had his gaze dragging itself from the glimpse of her thighs below the fall of pleats to the way her short jacket emphasized the nip of her waist and the generous swells of her breasts.

His inner Neanderthal instantly awoke. *Mine.*

Her features were mostly hidden by oversize sunglasses and a lipstick that had been applied to change the shape of her mouth. She pressed the door firmly closed behind her and stayed against it, hand on the latch.

"Hello." She leaned to set his room card on the nearby table. "Thank you for seeing me. I won't stay long."

She looked and sounded nervous, but he would swear her gaze was traveling all over him. He felt it as viscerally as the way her hands had skimmed across his skin when they'd last been in this room together.

Don't.

"Are you into role-play?" he drawled. "Is that why you're dressed like a hired assassin from a time-travel movie?"

"That's exactly what I am," she said without missing a beat. "I thought it would take more to convince you."

Damn. He didn't want to find her amusing. There was too much at stake.

"Take off your sunglasses. I want to see your face."

She complied, fumbling them slightly as she slipped them into a pocketbook hanging from a long strap over her shoulder. She lifted a frown of consternation to him.

"I actually made this for my interviews at—" She brushed the side of her skirt, making the pleats flutter. "Doesn't matter. I came to London to sell all the clothes I made, but I needed something to wear into this hotel that would blend in. I *am* a designer. I'm just not paid professionally for it."

"You're also a maid. Or you were, until they realized you have sticky fingers."

"It was *in* the *bin*," she said as though she was tired of repeating that. "Delia Chevron threw twenty-five thousand pounds *into the bin*. I thought it was a ticket for dinner and hoped to network or get some publicity for my work. Do you think at any point through all of this nightmare that one single pap has asked me who made my gown? Believe me, I've come to regret the whole escapade." She waved an arm in a wide circle.

"Me, too," he said, stung more deeply than he'd expected by that word *regret*.

She dropped her arm and her mouth pouted with injury, as though that particular word had landed just as hard for her.

Then she set her jaw and lifted her chin.

"Don't pin what happened onto me. I changed my mind

about that gala before you'd even spoken to me. You dragged me there, throwing me to them as 'fresh meat to chew on.' Do you know that I thought I was on a date?" She tapped where the pretty yellow lace of her camisole peeked between her lapels. "You might have explained that I was your *paid escort.* Who the hell sends a woman earrings worth a hundred and fifty thousand pounds for *one* night together? I wasn't that good, Saint."

He would beg to differ but only ran his tongue across his teeth.

"Why didn't you text me sooner?" he asked.

"Because you cost me my job and set the hounds of hell upon me. Thanks. Sign me up for more of that. I can't wait."

This was going well. He ran his hand down his face, trying to reset.

"I should have dealt with Julie sooner, instead of giving her an opportunity to feed off your story. That wasn't fair to you."

"You think?"

"Is that why you're here? To tell me you're angry at how this played out?" He would only grovel so far, and she'd just witnessed the extent of it. "Or have you decided you want compensation for your trouble after all?" He moved to the ice bucket. It held a bottle of Prieur Montrachet that he'd had room service deliver. "Have a seat. Do you want something to drink while we discuss terms?"

She didn't move.

He pulled the bottle from the ice and glanced over, catching a look of wounded shock on her face.

"That's really mean," she said.

"What is?"

Saint knew. He was uncomfortable with his guilt and how strongly he was reacting to her. He was doing what he'd learned to do when intense emotions took hold in him—he set them aside and used cold logic while he did whatever was necessary to make the issue go away.

"I can't undo what happened, Fliss. I did cost you your job and threw unwanted attention onto you. People seem to think I don't take responsibility for my actions, but I do." Money might not fix everything, but it bought some very effective bandages. "Tell me what will make you feel better, and I'll see what I can do. A storefront for a boutique perhaps?"

Still she didn't move or speak.

He opened the bottle and poured two glasses, then carried them to the coffee table.

"Come," he invited as he seated himself and leaned back.

After a moment, she came toward him. She seemed very pale as she sat on the sofa across from him, only lowering to perch on the edge of the cushion. She stared at the glass of wine but only clasped her hands in her lap, back very straight. She lifted her gaze to his.

"I didn't come here to ask anything of you," she said with quiet dignity. "Nothing. I mean that. *Nothing.*"

"Except my time," he noted drily.

"Not even much of that," she assured him with a proud lift of her chin. "I'm catching the train back to Nottingham once I've finished the rest of my errands. You'll never hear from me again. But I had to tell you something that didn't feel right to send as a text."

"What's that?" He did his best to sound detached, but his ears were ringing with that word. *Never.* He held his breath, straining to hear over that jarring sound of a train disappearing down a tunnel. His muscles felt both paralyzed and tense with readiness to leap and catch.

"I'm pregnant."

Saint didn't move. She wasn't sure he was breathing.

Then there was a faint, fractured clink before he gave his wine a startled look and swore.

He'd snapped the stem on his glass. He cupped one hand under the other and rose to head to the bar.

"Are you bleeding?" Fliss hurried after him to see him rinse the welling blood from his fingers into the sink. "I'll call the desk." She looked for the hotel phone.

"I can deal with it." He wrapped a clean bar towel around his fingers as he strode into the bedroom.

Fliss covered where her heart had been pounding with anxiety from the time she'd worked up the courage to hit Send on her text. It had increased to alarming levels when she had entered this hotel, picked up the card from a bored-looking bellman, then stepped off the elevator and made her way to this door. Now it was racing so fast she felt dizzy. Her nerve endings were sizzling and her mouth had gone dry.

Entering this suite was like stepping into a dream, but one of those weird ones that repeated every time you closed your eyes, the kind that made you feel stuck and fighting to wake up.

Everywhere she looked, sensual memories accosted her. She'd pressed her hands to that glass door and felt him inside her. He'd carried her through that doorway and stripped her naked, and they'd showered together before taking to the bed where they had touched and kissed each other *everywhere*. He had spoken wicked commands and reverent compliments in a sexy rasp.

Tell me if it's too much. I can't get enough of you.

As she had dressed to come here, she had braced for the impact of that potent sexuality of his. She had known she would react to his rangy, athletic body in his tailored trousers and crisp shirt. She had known she would want to push her fingers into his hair again, to press her mouth to his stern lips and nuzzle the scent in his throat.

She had not been prepared for his aloof, businesslike wall of commerce.

You want compensation after all?

She had suspected he would think that, but she hadn't expected it to stab so deeply to hear it.

"Are you sure it's mine? I used condoms."

She nearly leapt out of her skin, not realizing he'd come back. She grappled at the edge of the bar to steady herself, feeling spun around one too many times by all of this.

"Are you okay?" She looked to his hand. Two fingers wore beige-colored bandages.

"Fine." He folded his arms, feet braced. He'd withdrawn even further, presenting her with a wall of frost that chilled her to the bone. "This is why you're here, then? You think you've pulled the golden ticket?"

She opened her mouth, but her voice stalled in her throat. In her head, all her words had been carefully planned out, but none of this was going the way she'd expected. Her thoughts were scattered on the wind.

"This is not my first stroll around this particular block, Fliss." Saint's tone grew even more deep and lethal.

"Wh-what…?" She had to press her wobbling lips to-gether to make them work. "What do you do?"

"What do you mean?"

"When it's yours. What do you do?" She dropped her gaze to the elegant buckles on his shoes and the fine detail work across the toes, trying to tell herself that his skep-ticism worked in her favor. "You don't have any children that you acknowledge, so what do you do when it's yours? Pay for termination or—"

"They've never *been* mine." He spoke through his teeth. "If I had children, I'd acknowledge them, but I don't. That's why I wear condoms, so claims like this don't even arise. And I say this without judgment, Fliss…"

Oh, he was definitely judging her. She flashed a rancor-ous look up at him.

"I've seen what people have said about you online." His voice and expression were cool and remote. "I can't take your word for it that it's mine."

"Wow." She couldn't hide the slap of that. She looked away, unable to keep from revealing her torment. It wasn't just the memory of those old, cruel rumors. It was de-meaning enough that he knew about that time of her life. She couldn't believe he had thrown it in her face like that, though.

"I don't care how many lovers you've had," he said grimly. "I'm not that much of a hypocrite. I'm only saying I can't take it on faith that your baby is mine."

"You're—" She had to clear the thickness of humiliation from her throat. It came from realizing that she'd nurtured a barely acknowledged hope that this would go differently. Deep in her subconscious, she'd thought he might welcome her back into his life and greet this news with the joy that imbued her.

Fool. Struck by lightning. A new day. A naked child on a horse, proceeding into the future alone.

"You're making assumptions," she said, fighting to inject some semblance of dignity into her voice as she scraped for the words she'd come to say. "I only came to ask you to make a statement that it's *not* yours, so the paparazzi will leave me alone." She fumbled her sunglasses from her pocketbook and put them on before she looked at him again.

He was standing like a pillar, lips parted as though he'd been about to say something. His brows were a thick, foreboding line.

She wished these cheap lenses didn't afford him such a golden glow. He looked like a bronzed statue. A gleaming study in wrath.

"Will you?" she prompted, arteries stinging from the adrenaline running through them.

"It's not mine." Why did he sound so angered? Shouldn't he have been relieved? "That's why you came here today? To tell me it's *not* mine?"

"It seemed fair to warn you." Now the words she'd rehearsed were coming more easily. "It's all over the entertainment sites that you're looking for a wife. It would be awkward if rumors about me started while you were engaged to someone else, wouldn't it? Your intended would be dragged into something she didn't sign up for. I'd rather skip that myself, if you don't mind. So will you? Make a statement?"

"Take off those glasses." He was trying to pierce through their mirrored lenses with the strength of his glower.

"No." She stood straighter, chin up, but she was quivering like jelly inside.

"Is the baby mine or not, Fliss?"

"You wore condoms," she reminded him, refusing to outright lie. "None broke, did they?"

"No, but we had sex. There's a chance it's mine, isn't there? That's why you're here."

"With the legions of men I've entertained? Who's to say?" she said scathingly.

"Don't play games, Fliss."

"This isn't a game," she snapped. "I'm pregnant. The baby is mine. Your only obligation is to tell people to leave me alone. *That's* what I came to tell you today."

She headed for the door, but when she got there, he was there, too, covering the seam to keep it shut. He loomed so close around her she spun to face him, more angry than alarmed.

"Don't make this ugly," she said shakily.

He fell back a step and let his hand fall, but his jaw was clenched, his mouth tight.

"I want a paternity test."

"Why? You want this problem to go away. Let me go away." Fliss reached for the latch.

"So you can, what? Raise my child in some squalid flat on government handouts?"

"I would sell my diamond earrings, but I never received them, did I?" she shot back.

"You're still playing out of your league, Fliss." His hand came up to the door again, leaning on it. "I won't let you use my child against me."

Her heart had become a shriveled thing inside her, leaving a cavern for her voice to reverberate with emotion.

"Don't judge me by your standards, Saint. That's not something I would even think to do. I'm naive that way—which I'm pretty sure you know because I didn't feel played until I heard about those earrings. I thought you were charming and interesting and a generous lover. I thought we were two people who had a really nice time together, but you know which one of us was full of BS that night? You. It was all an act to get me into bed, wasn't it? And you think *I'm* into role-play?" She pointed between her breasts. "You're superficial and callous and kind of a bully. There's no way on *earth* I would raise a baby with you. Now, let me go before I scream the place down."

Fliss made to elbow him in the stomach, forcing him to step back to avoid it. She opened the door and left.

Saint had taken a kick from one of his mother's horses once. This was a similar sensation. He felt knocked clean across a stall.

He was vaguely aware of other sensations. His fingers were still stinging where he'd cut them with the glass. His blood felt thick and congealed in his veins, as though it was pooling in shock. His guts were pure acid.

It wasn't true, was it? There'd been a handful of paternity claims in his past. In the first case, he'd been young enough to buy in very quickly and had nearly bought his partner a ring, only to learn she wasn't even pregnant. Another time, he hadn't been the father.

Those false alarms had not only made him cynical about such claims but made him all the more diligent about wearing condoms. He bought them himself and regularly checked the dates. As Fliss had noted, none had split, so it seemed highly unlikely they had failed.

A compulsion to double-check the dates had him striding into the bathroom where his shaver was in its case. A half strip of condoms was tucked beside it, exactly the way he usually kept it. They were the brand he liked and part of the same strip he'd used with Fliss. The stamp said they were within their use-by date.

She'd been with him every second that night. There'd been no opportunity for her to poke holes in them—

He swore and crushed the strip in his fist, eyes pressing closed. *Fliss* hadn't had an opportunity to sabotage his birth control, but someone else had.

With a grim sense of premonition, he tore one out and sealed its opening to the tap. He filled it with water, then held it at his eye level and watched a droplet of water leak out against the skin. As soon as it fell, another formed. Then another.

With a curse, Saint threw the condom into the shower. It landed with a loud splat. He tried another. Then another. All of them were damaged.

Julie. He couldn't prove she was the one who had done it, but no one else had traveled with him and spent time in his space, and she'd already shown herself short on scruples.

At least he wasn't expecting a baby with *her*.

No. He was expecting one with Fliss.

You're superficial and callous and kind of a bully.

He drew in a breath that burned, hating himself for going full Ted Montgomery on her.

But this circumstance was *exactly* what his own father

had faced when Saint's mother had come to him with her unplanned pregnancy. Ted had been on the cusp of what had turned into unprecedented success. Norma had contributed to his ascension in no small way, not that Ted ever gave her that credit. Any warmth or charm that Saint possessed had come from her. She'd compensated for Ted's utter lack of empathy.

But such a one-sided relationship could only be sustained so long. Eventually, their marriage had become a toxic partnership, one that continued to rain nuclear fallout on Saint to this day.

That was why he wore condoms. He didn't want kids. He didn't want to discover thirty years from now that he was as damaging a parent as his own had been.

He was about to become one anyway. He didn't need a paternity test to prove it. He sent another dour look to the discarded condoms in the shower.

Fliss might have walked a very thin line between implying and outright lying about whether her baby was his, but he had no doubt that she was pregnant and that he had put her in that condition. He had even less doubt that she wished it had been nearly any other man.

This isn't a game, she'd said. *The baby is mine.*

Saint found himself thinking, *Mine, too.*

He braced his hands on either side of the sink, reminding himself to breathe while he took that in. Whether he wanted to be a father or feared he'd make a terrible one didn't matter. He was about to be put to the test. This was real. And he *did* take responsibility for his actions—even when his mistake was putting too much trust in the wrong person.

Swearing did nothing to help, but it felt very satisfying to curse out a long, vicious blue streak. Sensation was seeping back into his limbs, and his brain was crawling out of the rubble of emotions that were still piled up around him: shock and fury and guilt. So much guilt toward Fliss. There was something else there, too, deep under the heavy weight of that. Something that was too nascent to excavate. Something almost like relief or... He didn't know what it was and would rather focus on taking action.

He needed a paternity test for his father's sake. Ted would turn this into another black mark against Saint, possibly vetoing the board's approval.

Saint swore again, tiredly this time, and pinched the bridge of his nose.

You want this problem to go away. Let me go away.

As if it were that simple. She was right. As soon as she grew plump enough for people to suspect pregnancy, they would do the math and guess that he was the father. Even if he wanted to take the easy way out that she'd offered and made a statement that the baby wasn't his, she would still be badgered.

And he couldn't turn his back on his child. Not in good conscience. Within a year or two, the baby would look just like him anyway, giving how strongly he resembled his own father.

No, if Fliss was having his baby, *they* were having *their* baby.

Where had she said she was going? Errands. Hell. That could mean anything. If he wanted to catch her, he'd have to be waiting in Nottingham for her.

He went to look for his phone to order the car, ignoring the way Fliss's last words resounded in his ears.

There's no way on earth *I would raise a baby with you.*

CHAPTER SIX

WEEPING IN PUBLIC—on a train, for instance—was a skill Fliss had mastered years ago. As a teen, when she'd been a veritable outcast given the side-eye wherever she went, she had left most of her tears on her pillow. Later, though, when Granny had been struggling and Fliss had felt very helpless, she'd put on a brave face at home and let emotion overwhelm her when she'd been on the bus to work.

It was a matter of having a scarf or a handful of tissues at the ready and taking slow, careful breaths. She liked to wear earbuds so if someone asked with concern whether she was all right, she could claim to be listening to a very sad book. She always kept the sobbing very contained, not making a production of it. She simply let the pain wash over her and leak out her eyes.

Not that Saint deserved her tears. She wasn't crying over him anyway. She was crying over the fact that Granny and her baby would never meet. And because her memory of a magical night had been revealed to be smoke and mirrors. It had been sleight of hand that was akin to a lie. She felt like a sucker.

She was crying because even though she wanted her baby and knew that she would make this work, she was overwhelmed and scared. She didn't have a strong network of support. She had some loose friendships in London, all singletons who were living their single lives, and Mrs. Bhamra, who was healthy for her age but an octogenarian all the same.

Fliss would tell her eventually, but she didn't want to worry the woman. She would wait until she'd paid her back for loaning her the deposit on her bedsit—which was nicer than the one she'd had in London, *Saint*. It had a window onto a well-tended garden and a kitchenette and her own loo. Her landlords were a pleasant older couple who spent their days birdwatching and their evenings talking about it. The house was situated a short bus ride to her day job and a few blocks from the pub where she picked up shifts when she could.

As she approached the station, she mopped the last of her tears, half-thinking she should tell the pub she was available if they needed her to come in tonight, but she was exhausted—emotionally and physically. She had barely slept last night, knowing she would see Saint today, then she'd been up early to get into London.

Her day had been an endurance event of cleaning her room, selling what she could online, then taking the last of her handmade clothing to a nearby consignment shop. She'd had that awful meeting with Saint, then returned to the house to change and catch her housemates as they'd come home from work. She'd said her final goodbye and turned over her key.

The remnants of her time in London were now in a small backpack, a couple of cloth grocery bags and Mrs. Bhamra's rolling suitcase. Fliss might yet sell her sewing machine—

a professional-grade Juki—but Mrs. Bhamra had said she would take it as security against the money she'd loaned her, so Fliss was hanging on to it for now.

Wearily, she gathered everything as the train stopped and made her way to the curb.

She was comparing the cost of taking a ride share home against walking to the tram when a swanky black sportscar pulled up before her. The driver's door opened and Saint rose from behind the wheel.

He wore the same clothes as earlier but had added mirrored sunglasses and a leather jacket that made him look *Top Gun* sexy.

Drat. She'd left her sunglasses on the train. She looked back into the station but knew they were gone.

"I've been parked over there for thirty minutes. I was starting to think I'd missed you." He opened the boot.

"I thought I made it clear that your infamy is a liability for me. I don't want to be seen with you." Her heart was in her throat from more than alarm and surprise. What did it mean that he was here?

"So get in. No one will see you." He started to take her suitcase, then checked as he realized how heavy it was. "What the hell is in here? A body?"

"The last man who crossed me, yes." She stared into the two miniature reflections of her own glower.

"A woman in your condition ought to ask for help with heavy tasks like that," he said with false benevolence. "Good thing I'm here now."

"Lucky me." God, she hated him for the effortless way he set the rolling bag into the car. Her bags went in beside it.

She really wanted to tell him to go to hell, but she sank

into the passenger seat with a sigh of relief, then slouched low, peering out to see if anyone was pointing a phone their way.

The boot thumped closed, and Saint slid behind the wheel. "Where do you live?"

"Why are you here?" she asked at the same time.

"Why do you think?" he asked.

"You have an unquenchable thirst for sadism? Head north," she said as he pulled away from the curb.

"I checked the condoms. They all leak."

"Oh my God." She sat up, twisting to face him, crying with persecution, "I did *not* sabotage your condoms!"

"I know you didn't." He was maintaining an annoyingly dispassionate tone. "My life is full of vultures and sharks, Fliss. People want to take advantage of me all the time. Sometimes there's collateral damage."

"Who would do something like that?" she asked with astonishment, but she could guess. He seemed to have a talent for alienating the women he'd slept with. "Don't refer to my pregnancy that way," she added in a grumble, falling back into her seat. "It's gross."

"Collateral damage?" He slowed as traffic became congested and turned his head to give her a penetrating look. The turmoil in the dark depths of his eyes belied the remote tone he was using. "Why would you be offended? Unless you're admitting the baby is mine?"

She bit her thumbnail and looked out her side window. "You're going to take the second exit after this one."

Aside from directions, they didn't talk again until he pulled into the cul-de-sac below the cozy brick house situated on a terraced lawn above them. It was accessed by a flight of stone steps cut into the retaining wall.

"You were going to carry this bag up these stairs?" Saint asked with disapproval as he took them from the boot and carried them himself.

"Is it too heavy for you? I can take it." The machine was twelve kilos, and she moved it around all the time, admittedly with an "Oof" of effort every time.

He didn't set the case on its rollers for the uneven path alongside the house to the back porch. He carried it to the door she unlocked, then brought it inside.

"Leave it down here," she said as she started up the narrow, creaking stairs. "I was going to take it to Mrs. Bhamra's on my way home. Now I'll have to do that tomorrow."

"Who's Mrs. Bhamra?" He followed her into the converted attic and looked around.

The single bed was under the lowest side of the slanted ceiling, but Fliss was still able to sit up without smacking her head. There was a bistro table that looked out the dormer window. A four-drawer bureau supported the microwave. There was a mini fridge and two-burner stovetop in the kitchenette, and open shelving displayed her handful of dishes and dry goods.

"Tea?" she offered because she could tell she wouldn't get away with offering him a tip for his chauffeur duties and holding the door for him to leave.

"Coffee?" he countered. "Something stronger?" He was looking at the sketchbook she'd left on the table where she had scrawled out ideas for adding maternity panels to some of her existing clothes.

"You've come to the wrong place for caffeine and alcohol."

"Right." He lifted his head. "How is everything? Have you seen a doctor?"

"Yes." She'd had a scan a week ago, wanting to be sure everything was okay before she'd contacted him. It was.

She filled the kettle and set it to boil.

"I need to hear you say it, Fliss." He stood with his hands hooked into his pockets, his expression mostly hidden behind his sunglasses.

He'd been right—it was annoying to try to read someone when they were wearing such an impervious shield.

"What?" She played dumb.

"Tell me it's mine."

She took off her light jacket and hung it on the hook by the door, ignoring his request because it felt too much like relinquishing what little agency she had.

"Why are you here?" she asked instead.

"You're having my baby. We have things to talk about."

"Like the fact that you have put me in the impossible position of being either an unfit mother who can only afford a bedsit." She waved at her humble home. "Or a parasite who regards her child as a meal ticket?"

He looked to the window, profile carved from granite except for the way his cheek ticked.

"Are you hungry?" she asked. "Mrs. Bhamra gave me butter chicken when I picked up the case yesterday. There's lots."

"No, thank you. Who is she? Your landlady?"

"A friend of Granny's. I should text her, actually, so she knows I'm back safe." It was nice to have someone worrying about her again. She texted, then started to scoop the cold chicken and rice into a bowl.

"You don't have to eat leftovers. I'll buy you dinner. Where do you want to go?"

"Nowhere. I'm tired." She set the bowl into the microwave and started it, then finished making the tea. In her mind, she heard Granny gasp in horror that she dropped a pair of teabags straight into cups, but she didn't actually own a teapot anymore. The one that had been Granny's had broken—along with her heart—ages ago. She'd never replaced it.

Fliss carried the cups to the table and left them there while she closed her sketchpad and moved it with the pencils to the bed.

"What do you know about me?" Saint asked. "What have you heard or read?"

"Are you asking how much I've stalked you online? I didn't have to. We were mentioned in the same articles. Although I had to quit reading once I got the gist that I'm a penniless, thieving whore. Better that than a philandering billionaire sociopath, I always say."

He swore under his breath and removed his sunglasses to push a finger and thumb against the inside corners of his eyes.

"Oh, am I supposed to tell you what I've read, not what I know?" she asked without heat. "You're famous for being rich and good-looking. Your father invented a microchip or something. Your mother was a prize model on a game show. That was all before my time, so I don't know much about either of them. Celebrity trivia isn't something I follow. Unless it's fashion related, but even at that I was fifteen when I said to Gran, 'Did you know Stella McCartney's father is a famous musician?' I didn't know who the Beatles were, only that Stella's work was fur-free and leather-free. I knew which of her gowns had been on which red carpets. I know your shoes are Ferragamo and your shirt is Tom Ford. Trousers are a private tailor, I'm guessing. Jacket is Gucci, obviously."

He'd hung it on the chair back, and she could read the tag inside the collar.

"That's kind of impressive." He sounded sincere.

"It's not. All it really tells me is that you're rich and have decent taste." The microwave dinged, so she brought her dinner to the table.

"That smells really good."

"Take this one."

He shook his head, waving at her to eat as he seated himself across from her, but sat sideways in the chair. He braced his back against the wall and hooked his arm over the railed back of the chair. His other arm rested flat on the table.

"My father came from oil money," he said. "His father was a mean drunk, and Dad's three older brothers were cut from the same cloth. Toxic masculinity is their default." He gave a curl of his lip. "None of them saw any value in my father's passion for computers. My grandfather forced Dad to take business courses and put him in sales, which was the worst possible place for him. As soon as the old man died, he had his brothers buy him out and used the money to develop his microchip. It was a hit."

"Are his brothers nicer to him now?"

"They might be if Dad was nicer to them." Saint played with the handle on his teacup. "Growing up, Dad was the quintessential nerd—before it was cool to be one," he added dourly. "Once Grayscale took off, he was all business. The cutthroat kind. He moved to California and began eating start-ups. He discovered that having money made him very attractive, too. Name a starlet from the eighties and there's probably a photo of him with her."

That actually sounded like a fun game, but Saint kept talking, not giving her a chance to play.

"He met Mom at a party. Like most of his dates at the time, she was quite a bit younger than him, very glamorous looking, but she was straight off the farm in Iowa. Their affair didn't last long. She came with her own baggage, stuff she never talks about. She told me once she was looking for someone who would make her feel safe. Dad was already in his forties, swimming in money, but he'd never been married or had any long-term relationships. At first, she thought he was shy, but it turns out he's withdrawn and incapable of meaningful connection. She broke it off, then she found out she was pregnant."

"Oh?" This story was sounding uncomfortably familiar. He nodded slowly, not looking at her.

"Dad's friends—advisors, I should call them. They knew he was still on an upward trajectory and had their own reasons for wanting to protect their stake in that. They told him to pay Mom off. She convinced Dad that I deserved to know my father. What if I was a boy? Wouldn't I inherit the company? Shouldn't he raise me to take it over?"

"Sexist. What if you were a girl?"

"Tip of the iceberg," he dismissed with a flick of his fingers. "Mom wanted to keep working. Dad said no. He wanted a trophy wife, one who would smile as she stood next to all the great things he made to improve the world."

"Like you?"

He made a noise of grim amusement. "I stopped trying to be his pride and joy long ago," he admitted drily. "I watched Mom do it for too long and realized it's a lost cause."

"Are they still married?"

"Yes. At first she stayed for me. And because she wanted more children. She didn't want to fail," he added with a wince of understanding. "No one does. But while they were pretending to make it work, Dad had a string of affairs and Mom had three miscarriages. Their prenup was weighted heavily in Dad's favor if she left him. She might not have married him for his money, but she contributed enough to his success that she feels entitled to a bite of it. She could embroil him in a big, ugly divorce if she wanted to, but she doesn't have his level of ruthless disregard and he knows it. It's become a marriage based on spite."

"Family dinners must be fun." Fliss poked at a chunk of chicken, having lost her appetite.

"They're a nightmare," he assured her. "Dad says it doesn't make financial sense to give her half his fortune when I'll only inherit from both of them. It's better to keep it whole. That's his way of claiming he's being stubborn for me. It's not for me." Saint shook his head. "He fears that she'd come after shares in the company. If she got them, he wouldn't have majority control any longer."

"What's your relationship with him like?"

"Terrible," he said conversationally. "But I will inherit Grayscale eventually, and I do want it. I don't overlook what it cost my parents to create this titan of the industry, but I also think, why? Why suffer that long, hating your partner, only to demand I be grateful for their sacrifice?

Mom has her horses and Dad has his coven of toadies who scurry around telling him how smart he is, but is that really enough to compensate for all those years of being cruel to each other?"

"When they could have parted and found love elsewhere?"

"When they could have not actively hated each other. I don't understand it. I really don't." He picked up his cup and brought it to his lips but didn't sip. "I only knew that I never wanted to lock myself into a lifetime of the same thing."

Ah. Fliss had wondered why he was telling her all of this.

"I don't expect you to marry me, Saint," she said quietly, ignoring the way her heart felt pinched in a vise.

"I know," he said simply, causing her pulse to lift and dip as she felt understood and believed but also rebuffed. Then his arrow-sharp gaze hit her. "I still have to."

CHAPTER SEVEN

"No, you don't!" Fliss sat back in shock. "You just gave me a great reason why marriage is a terrible idea. All you have to do is say the baby isn't yours and walk away."

Saint finished lifting his cup to his lips, but his mouth wasn't prepared for whatever this was. It was hot like coffee but weak. It had the color and bitterness of scotch but no bite. He didn't think he'd had a sip of tea in his adult life. Not since he'd tried the stuff as a child and decided he didn't like it.

He still didn't. He set it aside with distaste.

"I don't have the words to express how insulted I am by your thinking I would deliberately reject my child." Especially when he'd just explained how unenthusiastically he'd been welcomed by his own father.

Saint held her wide-eyed stare for a full thirty seconds, until she dropped her gaze to her curry and rice. Then her brows lifted in a silent, cynical *Whatever*.

He was deeply insulted but also uneasy. He *had* put her in an impossible position.

Her bedsit was tiny and definitely inadequate for raising a child. The stairs alone were a guaranteed trip to the hospital, but as humble as this space was, she'd made it homey. It was tidy and organized and more colorful and welcoming than any home he'd ever occupied. Her bedspread was a kaleidoscope of fabric scraps he would bet she had quilted herself. There were doilies in psychedelic spirals under her handful of houseplants. The frame on the photo over the sink was pebbled with a mosaic of what looked like broken china plates.

The photo inside it showed Fliss with her arm around an elderly woman he presumed was her grandmother, judging by the resemblance around their eyes and smiles. Saint had the unnerving feeling that the old woman was watching him from that photo, judging him.

"The baby has become my top priority." He'd had ample time while driving from London to let this situation sink in. He'd already projected through his father's reaction and how this could impact the board's decision. The gossip sites would have a field day, which would affect Fliss and, in turn, their baby. "That makes you my top priority. Your health and safety. I have to look after you, Fliss."

Did her eyes gloss with tears? If they did, she hid it by taking her empty bowl to the sink where she kept her back to him while she rinsed the dish.

"I said some unkind things back at the hotel," he acknowledged. "I was taught to go on the attack when I feel threatened."

"I wasn't threatening you." She turned and crossed her arms, leaning her hips against the front of the sink. "I gave you information."

"I know. I see that now." He was still on the defensive, this time in a different way. It still made him uneasy and caused him to prickle with aggression. "What's important for you to hear is that I don't want my child raised in the sort of atmosphere I grew up in. I won't be so hard on you again," he vowed. "I know you'll hold me to account on that."

"That's not my job. Hold yourself to account."

"I am," he said drily. "That's why I'm here."

She *tsked* and frowned at the foot of her bed. She had changed into jeans and a T-shirt before catching the train. Her faded yellow shirt hung loose over her waistband, so he couldn't tell if her waist was thickening, but he would swear her breasts were fuller than the already deliciously round swells he had worshipped so thoroughly three months ago.

He swallowed, trying not to get distracted with memories.

"We have to try, Fliss. I live a very good life. One that our child is entitled to. I can offer *you* a very good life." He glanced toward the sketchbook, impressed with her flare for a graceful line and a pop of unexpected color or pattern. "Are you really going to put your dreams on hold for the next eighteen years? I can help you achieve them, you know."

"Ew! It's not an achievement if someone hands it to you."

Was that a dig at what he stood to inherit?

"It's not cheating to maximize the opportunities you're given. Try telling me that Ms. McCartney's last name didn't open doors for her. Tell me that growing up in a world where she already had access to designers and celebrities didn't give her a leg up. That's all I'm offering you."

"That's not why I'm having this baby, though," Fliss blurted. "I need you to hear that and believe it."

"Why, then?" he asked, more from curiosity than suspicion.

The tendons in her neck briefly stood out, as though his question put her under great stress. When she spoke, her voice was quiet and held an ache that penetrated far more deeply into him than was comfortable.

"I don't have anyone anymore. Granny is gone and..." She waved toward the photo of her grandmother. "I want a family, even if it's just me and my one child. I don't want whatever it is that you just described." Her splayed hand drew a circle to encompass the conflict that had been baked into his upbringing. "That sounds awful."

"Understood." He didn't blame her for resisting an invitation into his family, but he didn't regret warning her what it was like, either. She needed to know where he'd come from and what she was getting into. "You didn't intend to get pregnant. I know that."

He was heartened by what he perceived as genuinely sentimental feelings toward their baby, too. They didn't keep a jaded part of him from remaining on guard against her, though, speculating whether her show of reluctance to marry was a long con of some kind. He wasn't forgetting about that invitation she'd taken.

All of that aside, however. "We can still make the best of an unexpected situation."

"A rush into marriage is not 'the best.'" She was still hugging herself, shoulders high and tense, brow crinkled with consternation.

"We don't have to marry right away. At least come home with me—"

"To America? I can't leave my life here!"

What life? He bit back the question, rephrasing to a milder,

"What would you be leaving behind that you can't live with-out?"

"Mrs. Bhamra," she mumbled, biting her thumbnail.

"I come to London constantly. I've actually debated buy-ing a property here. We could do that so we have more of a home here."

"So I'd live in London and you'd come and go?"

"New York is a more convenient base for me because I fly to LA as often as anywhere else. Let's start in New York while we figure out how to live together. Ultimately, we'll settle wherever we decide is best for our baby to live."

"I don't have health insurance in America."

"That's not even an argument. I'll fund an obstetrics wing if I have to."

She rolled her eyes. "Must be nice."

"It is. Try it," he said blithely.

Her mouth pursed in dismay.

"What would that even look like? Would we live as roommates or…?" Her tone was overly casual, but he could see how hard she was trying to sound blasé when she glanced at him. Apprehension had stiffened her expression.

He let his head thump back against the wall, watching her through the screen of his lashes. "Is that what you'd prefer?"

Fliss seemed to find something extremely interesting on the side of her elbow. "Well, it's not as if we were planning to continue our affair, is it?"

"I was."

Her gaze clashed with his.

"What do you think the earrings were for?" he chided.

"You tell me. Do you regularly give women such outra-geous gifts for a night of sex?"

Saint drew a breath that seared his lungs with fresh liability. She was too good at prying into him, forcing him to self-exam and see where he fell short.

"My relationships have always been superficial," he admitted, rising in a restless attempt to dodge that spiky truth. "You weren't wrong when you called me that. And, as you've discovered, my life can be taxing on those who get involved with me, even briefly. If I can reduce the criticism or soften the impact, I do."

"With jewelry? Just admit you're paying for sex, Saint. This is a safe space. No judgment." She sounded facetious.

"I'm paying for the fact that I don't offer much beyond sex," he prevaricated. "I'm monogamous and materially generous, but I don't fall in love. Emotions are grit in my teeth. That's why I have the reputation I do, so no one expects grand gestures or heartfelt declarations."

"You should be in sales. I can't wait to overturn my life for that."

"You're doing it for our child."

"Right. It's not about me." Her voice sounded tight.

"I'm aware of my limitations, Fliss. Now you are, too. We're going into this with a much clearer vision than my parents had. My mother mistook passion for love and didn't understand why it faded. You won't have those sorts of unrealistic expectations of me."

"And what would you expect of me?" she challenged, expression cantankerous.

"I'd *like* sex, but I don't expect it, if that's what you're asking."

"No—" She made an impatient noise. He didn't think she could hug herself any harder without turning herself inside out. "According to the headlines, you're looking to settle down with 'someone who shares your values.' That's not me. I know that because it's been three months without a word from you. You didn't even ask me to continue that affair you claim to have wanted. Don't—" She held up a stalling finger. "Don't say you didn't have my number. If you can get Delia Chevron's personal number, you can get mine. You're only here—" she pointed at the floor "—because *I* came to *you*. So don't pretend you want *me* when what you really want is sex. If you want honesty between us, be honest about that."

Saint rocked back on his heels, annoyed that she was such a pugnacious fighter but admiring how tough she was at the same time.

"My search for a wife is a smoke screen. I was generating too much unflattering publicity. The board refused to fund an important project until I was able to prove I take Grayscale and my future seriously. Much as I wanted to call you, I thought it was better to let the attention die down."

"And your silence had nothing to do with finding out I was a lowly housemaid." Her words dripped cynicism.

"The part where you were fired for theft concerned me," he said with gravity. "Not the job you were doing at the time."

Fliss dropped her gaze, not bothering to make more excuses.

"Now you be honest," he commanded gruffly. "Would you have continued our affair if I'd asked?"

"I don't know." She was staring into a corner, profile tortured.

"Really?" The tension of expecting a blow came into his abdomen. "Do you not think of that night as often as I do?"

Her gaze swept to his, wide with exposure, then slid to

the bed before snapping away. The flush of pink that came into her cheeks was so ripe with sensual reminiscence he had to fight a smug smile of gratification.

"Okay, then." All he wanted in that moment was to crawl onto that narrow mattress with her and relive every single thing they'd done. Then start making new memories.

"What 'okay'? No. All I'm hearing is that you need a trophy wife," she blurted. "How do you expect an unplanned pregnancy with a scrounging housemaid will go over with your board?"

"Oh, they'll treat it like a national holiday. There might even be a parade."

"Gawd," she cried softly and buried her face in her hands.

"Fliss." He couldn't resist going over to take her hands, forcing her to reveal all the uncertainty gripping her. "I've already thought through how I'll handle it. And once everyone realizes I'm producing Theodore the Third, they'll be very happy for us."

She quirked her brow. "Is your real name Theodore?"

"Now you know my deep dark secret," he said. "Why are you shaking your head? You think our baby is a girl? Gender is a construct."

"Because you're moving too fast, Saint Theodore." She shook her hands free of his.

"Theodore Saint Garvey Montgomery," he clarified. "And what about your experience with me makes you think I move any other way?"

"I thought you wanted a paternity test?" She paced back to the table. "Let's both take a beat while we wait for the results. After that, if we decide to try—" her voice faltered "—living together, I'll give notice at work."

"Do you really doubt that I'm the father?" he asked with a frown.

"I thought you did."

He chewed the corner of his mouth, thinking about the way she'd flinched when he'd said back at the hotel that he couldn't take her word for it.

"My father will want one, but you and I need to be able to trust each other, so tell me the truth—I swear I won't be angry. Is there someone else who could be the father?"

She flinched again, making him want to probe why, but after a moment of hesitation, she pressed her lips together and shook her head, conceding, "You're the only person I've been with."

"Good." A strange sensation washed through him. It was something like relief and something like elation. It sank so deeply into him, it crept toward places he guarded very closely, threatening to get under the door.

"How is that good?" Fliss asked skeptically.

"You're being honest with me. That's very good." He was side-stepping what she had really asked so he didn't have to explain his inexplicable reaction. He was far more comfortable with stepping into action. "Now, you said yourself that you'll be showing soon, so let's get ahead of this. Come to New York with me, and we'll let people see we're in a relationship. We'll announce the baby news when we can no longer hide it." He took out his phone to text Willow. "What's evening traffic like? Is it realistic that we could be at the airport in two hours?"

"*No.* I just finished bringing my things from London. I

can't pack up my life again in ten minutes. Where would I even put it?"

"I genuinely don't understand the question." He searched Fliss's distressed expression, trying to see the problem. "I'll pay the rent here until we find a place in London, then I'll hire movers to bring all of this there. Pack what you want with you in New York, which I presume is that photo of Granny and your tarot cards. Text your employer that you quit. We'll say goodbye to Mrs. Bhamra on the way out of town."

Fliss was on Saint's private jet before she had fully absorbed what she had agreed to do, but it was too late for all the qualms that piled on her with the climb in altitude.

This was the real fall from the Tower, she realized. She was literally in the air, the life she'd built, such as it was, falling away. She didn't even have a job to go back to. She had a few hundred pounds in the bank and Mrs. Bhamra's insistence that she should call if she needed anything.

As they reached cruising altitude, the flight attendant offered drinks and asked if they would like her to prepare their meal.

"I've eaten, thanks," Fliss said, stifling a yawn.

"I'll eat later." Saint frowned with concern at her. "Are you tired?"

She'd nodded off in the car on the drive to the airport, so she ought to have had a little more in her, but, "I was up really early this morning, and it was a long day. I wouldn't mind shutting my eyes for a bit." Plus, she needed time to process all that had happened.

"Use the bed." He unclipped his seat belt and rose. "Come. I'll show you."

It was a throwaway comment. He didn't mean he'd show her how to use the bed, but he sure had the last time they'd been together. As she followed him to the back of the cabin, her cheeks stung with self-conscious heat.

"Are you blushing?" he asked in an amused undertone as he held the door for her.

"Don't tease." She covered her hot cheeks.

"This from the woman who showed up in a schoolgirl skirt today?"

"You said I looked like an assassin," she said over her shoulder.

"The sexy kind from the free-love era. I was looking forward to engaging in hand-to-hand combat, but you got the advantage over me in other ways."

She lost her sense of humor as she moved further into the stateroom. Like the rest of the jet, it was decorated in earthy colors and textures. The head of the bed was a huge, illuminated panel with the silhouette of bamboo plants cast from the backside, giving the impression the forest was just beyond a translucent window. Lamps stood on night tables made of faux granite, and the walls were paneled in mahogany.

"That was a joke," he said in a low voice.

"I know." But it was actually bothering her that she stood to gain anything from this baby, even a free flight to America. She had a dream, but she also had a heavy not-good-enough complex, thanks to years of stumbles and false starts. Shortcuts didn't win. She'd learned that with the invitation debacle.

While she peered into the luxurious bathroom, Saint pressed a louvered panel, opening it to reveal drawers. He pulled blue satin pajamas from one and tossed them onto the bed.

"Oh. Um—"

"For you. I told them not to bother unpacking your suitcase." His eyes were laughing at her again. "You're tired, so I wasn't planning to join you, but I am absolutely open to an invitation if you do want company."

He had told her he wanted sex but didn't expect it. She thought it was pretty obvious that she did expect it. Why else would she have agreed to go to New York with him? Yes, they had things to discuss about the baby, but she could have put her foot down.

She hadn't because she had known from the moment she'd awakened in his bed three months ago that she would like to continue waking beside him. She'd been furious and upset with him when their brief involvement had forced her to flee London, but a barely acknowledged possibility had been dancing in her mind from the time she'd discovered she was pregnant. Their baby had given her a reason to see him and *see*. At her latest checkup, she had asked her doctor if she could have sex. She'd shaved her legs yesterday, knowing she would see him today.

But there was that other tender part of her that had taken a fresh hit when their brief association had turned her into a punchline again.

As Fliss bit her lip and stared at the pajamas with indecision, he said, "No? That's fine." He started to the door.

That hurt, too, that he was able to take it or leave it so

casually when she was in such turmoil over whether to have
sex and what it might cost her.

Ugh. If she didn't tell him now, she never would.

"Saint."

He paused. His expression was infinitely patient, but her
heart started to beat faster. She swallowed, but the tension
in her lungs remained.

"I think you should know that..." She looked past him
to the door, feeling trapped, but even if she left this bedroom, she'd still be on a plane, thirty thousand feet over the
Atlantic. "When I said I hadn't been with anyone else..."

He didn't move, didn't say a word, but she sensed his
withdrawal. It was as though his body condensed into ice,
dropping the temperature in the room.

"It's not what you're thinking." She scrunched herself
into the corner beside the night table. "I mean, you probably thought I meant I hadn't been with anyone lately and
that's true, but you're actually only the second person I've
ever been with. The first was six—no, seven?—years ago."
She winced with apprehension as she said it.

His brows crashed together as he tried to fit that detail
into what he thought he knew about her.

"My...um...first boyfriend was mean to me."

"In what way?" The gritty danger that entered his tone
sent a chill down her spine.

"Not violent. Just...unkind. He pressured me to have
sex with him even though I was on the fence about it. It
wasn't assault." Fliss waved her hand, trying to forestall
whatever masculine aggression was building behind that
glowering, granite expression. "It was my choice but an
immature one. I thought he wouldn't like me anymore if

I didn't, and I wanted to find out what was so great about it. I didn't get much of an answer," she said in an aside of annoyed disgust.

"It was uncomfortable and unsatisfying. Maybe it would have gotten better with time. With someone else." She folded her arms. "But I didn't want to be intimate again because after we did it, he started bragging around school about it. I got mad and broke up with him, and he retaliated by telling everyone he had dumped me because I was giving it away to anyone who asked. I was only in our social group because I was with him. He was very popular, so when it came to picking sides, everyone chose the stud who'd been wronged over the slut who lied about it."

Saint muttered a curse under his breath, eyes closing. "Then you had sex with me, and..."

"Yeah. That ruined a really nice night." Her throat tightened, thinning her voice. Her chest was burning with self-consciousness. "I hadn't felt like that with him. Like I really wanted sex." *Needed* it. "I knew it would only be one night, but you seemed to know what you were doing and you were nice about it. You said we could stop if I wanted to. I thought it would be cathartic and something that was just for me. And you, obviously, but a nice memory that would replace my old one."

Saint's mouth was tight as he tracked his concerned gaze all over her. "I should have done more to protect you."

"Oh, you think?" She couldn't help her exasperated guffaw over that one.

"From the press," he clarified, mouth sliding sideways with self-deprecation. "But yeah. Physically, too."

"I didn't tell you that to put a guilt trip on you." She

looked to the bed and the pajamas, barely resisting the urge to pick them up and press her nose into the cool satin to see if she could smell his aftershave. "I was trying to say that yes, I want to sleep with you, but I'm also scared of what comes after, if things don't work out between us."

"It will work out." He came close enough to cup her elbows and draw her from the corner so she was right in front of him. "I'll make sure of it."

CHAPTER EIGHT

SAINT SPOKE AS though he meant it, so Fliss smiled as though she believed him.

Besides, she was growing overwhelmed by his closeness. Her hand found its way to his chest without her realizing it. Her fingertips tucked themselves behind the placket of his shirt between two buttonholes, and she tugged him closer while she lifted her mouth.

His breath hissed in at her unhesitating invitation. His head dipped, and his firm lips angled across hers.

At first contact, a sensual jolt pulsed through her, so strong it made her groan at the sting of it. Who cared if her life was destroyed by this? Touching him *was* life. He was hot and dynamic and pulsing with energy that shimmered into her, making her feel surrounded and safe and more alive than she ever had.

For three long months, she had been waiting to feel this way again, convinced she never would, but now she was back in this wondrous place where his lips moved over hers with controlled mastery. His palm slid up her arm to the back of her neck, cupping her head while he deepened the kiss at an achingly slow pace.

It was both soothing and inciting. Frustrating. Urgency

was rising in her, making her run her hands around to his back so she could pull herself tighter against him.

"I was an animal last time," Saint said, drifting his kiss to her cheek and brow. "You should have told me how long it had been. I would have been more careful."

"I liked it." He'd made her feel irresistible, and she wanted that rush again, maybe to reassure herself it was still there. Or that she held some of the power over him that he had implied, but even though she arched to press her pelvis into the stiffness behind his fly, he only made a sound of gratification and dragged at her hair so he could nuzzle his mouth against her throat.

"I've thought about you a lot. About that night." His free hand skimmed the side of her breast, then climbed beneath the fall of her T-shirt to trace patterns against her waist and lower back, showering her with tingling sensations. "About all the things I would do with you if I ever got the chance again." His hot words stimulated the hollow beneath her ear and stirred the fine hairs at her hairline. "The list is long, Fliss. Very, very long."

She was hearing him on a subliminal level, all her senses drawing tight with anticipation while he only teased her with the brush of his lips on her throat and the unhurried movement of his hand creeping higher and higher toward her breast. By the time his thumb traced the under-band of her bra, she was trembling.

But Fliss had the wherewithal to say, "Don't wreck it. I made it."

He lifted his head. "This?" His clever fingers grew more exploratory, making her wriggle when his tickling touch went into her armpit.

"Yes. And you ripped the knickers I made—"

"I wanted to *keep* them, they were so sexy. Let me see." He took hold of the hem of her T-shirt, forcing her to raise her arms, then skimmed it off and away. His gaze glittered with approval as he took in the jewel-colored scraps of silk, silver lace and black satin straps. "You made this?"

"I had to. I've already gone up a cup size."

"Hell yes, you have."

"Don't look too closely." Fliss touched a tiny wrinkle in the lace edging. "It's full of mistakes. Lingerie is very finicky and unforgiving."

"I'm looking very closely and all I see is perfection," he assured her in a throaty voice. "You should make nothing but lingerie. This is…" Saint slid his finger under the strap where it came over the top of her shoulder. It connected to an eyelet that supported a split strap that framed the upper swells of her breasts in bold triangles before connecting to either side of the balconette cups. He swallowed. "Magnificent."

The feathery trace of his touch was making her breasts tingle and swell. They ached, but even though she drew a breath and shifted, he showed no mercy. His thumb grazed the point of her nipple where it was lifting the amethyst silk.

She didn't realize she'd made a throaty noise until he paused. "Hurt?"

"No. It feels really good." Everything about his hands on her felt really, really good.

A satisfied rumble sounded in his throat. He brushed the strap off her shoulder, then scooped his hand inside the cup to dislodge it. His head ducked and he licked at her nipple, teasing, blowing softly, before he opened his mouth to take the tip deeply into the wet heat of his mouth. He sucked until she was standing on her tiptoes, fist knotted in his hair.

When Saint straightened, his eyes were glazed with lust. He checked in with her very briefly before he freed her other breast and bent her over his arm. He ravished the other one just as thoroughly, sending runnels of heat into her loins and making her cling and arch higher into his mouth and gasp his name.

He didn't let up. No, he pushed his hand into her jeans and knickers and discovered exactly how profound an effect he was having on her. She groaned with aching delight as the restriction of her clothes firmed his touch against her folds. His finger probed, and the plane of his palm sat implacably against the pulsing knot of nerves that had been waiting for this. For him.

"Saint." She was so aroused she was begging, bowed in supplication, lifting her hips to deepen his penetration, trying to increase the friction.

He fluttered his tongue against her nipple, and she lost it. Climax rippled through her, deep and satisfying, tearing a cry from her throat. If he hadn't held her so firmly, she would have fallen down as she fell apart. It was terrifying and exalting and left her so shaken she was still quivering when he removed his hand from her jeans and eased her onto the bed.

"I thought my memory had exaggerated how responsive you are," he said in a rasp. "Are you sure this is okay? I didn't expect you to come so hard and fast." He opened his hand across her abdomen where her muscles were still twitching in the aftermath.

He didn't look *that* worried. He looked kind of smug.

"It's very okay," she said shakily, opening her jeans and lifting her hips to push them down and off with the rest of her remaining clothes.

Saint straightened to yank at his own shirt and pants, his impatience flattering. His erection sprang forth. All of him was like burnished oak, carved and sanded into smooth planes and lovingly accentuated details. He swept his hand across his torso as he looked at her, then slid his hand down, taking hold of himself in a tight fist, expression tense with carnal hunger. He reached for the night table drawer.

"You don't need a condom," she reminded him. "Unless there are other issues? I had a full screen as part of my checkup."

"I was tested…" He frowned in recollection. "It was right before I left for London for the gala. There hasn't been anyone else since. I've never had sex without a condom, though."

"Me, neither. We're both virgins." Fliss sat up to draw the blankets down so she could get under them but paused to ask with false concern, "Do you think we should discuss it first? With a responsible adult we trust?"

"Like who? The pilot?" He threw the covers away and loomed over her, nipping at her lips with his own as he pressed her to the mattress. "Damn, but I've been wanting this."

"I thought about you a lot, too," she confessed in a whisper, stroking her hands down his strong back and over his firm buttocks.

Somehow, he made her feel both delicate and vulnerable but safe. He was proprietary in the way he inserted his legs between hers, effortlessly pushing hers open in a demonstration of how much strength he had—plenty enough to overpower her if he wanted to. But the way he kissed her was a coax.

Let me in. Come with me down this erotic path.

And he went down an erotic path of his own, one that took him over the hills of her breasts and across the field of her abdomen, then into the grove between her thighs.

"You don't have to—" She was already aroused enough, but her voice turned to a moan of indulgence.

"I really do," he said in a low voice, bringing his thumb into play with his tongue.

Fliss couldn't talk after that. All her brain cells were fried by the lazy way he was pulling her toward orgasm again, coiling sensation upon sensation until she was at the tipping point.

"Not yet, lovely," he said, lifting his head and stroking his thumb in the moisture of her folds, avoiding where she most needed to be caressed. "Wait for me."

He set his teeth against her inner thigh just tight enough to threaten pain, then sucked a love bite onto her skin. The discomfort drew her back from the edge but made her sob in denial.

"Soon," he crooned, climbing his wicked mouth over the wobbling muscles of her belly and pausing to worship her breasts once more. The inferno in her loins grew to an ache she couldn't bear.

"You're mean," she accused, so tense with need she thought she'd break in half.

"So mean," he agreed, taking his time with departing from her nipples before he finally, finally rose over her and guided himself to the molten core of her. "I'm going to savor this," he said in sinful warning. "But let me feel it, Fliss. Let me feel you come as many times as you can."

She was still very much out of her league, she realized in those seconds. Not just at his mercy, but willing to do anything for him. For this, the press of his thick shape sinking into her primed, welcoming sheath. Glorious shivers of near climax sent hot-cold sensations across her skin. Her knees bent to hug his sides and her heels dug into his ass, pressing him deeper.

Saint began to move, slow and deep and powerful, and it was all she needed. She twisted beneath him as orgasm detonated within her. Wild noises left her. Breath and thought and any sense of self were all gone in those moments of pure pleasure. Pure being.

"Beautiful," he murmured, sounding barely affected despite destroying her. He continued moving in those precise but leisurely thrusts. "Now another," he commanded, hooking his arm behind her knee to increase the depth of his possession.

She gave him everything he asked for.

"I don't want earrings," Fliss murmured through the dark, hours later, when they were exhausted and damp and drifting off to sleep.

Saint had her spooned into his front. He roused slightly, his ingrained cynicism thinking, *Here we go.*

"What would you prefer?"

"Respect." She sighed and snuggled deeper into his chest. Her hand slid to cover the one he had draped over her waist and grew heavy.

Seconds later, he could tell by the shallowness of her

breathing that she was deeply asleep, but he was wide awake, blinking into the darkness, aware of the white noise of the plane's engines and an itch against his conscience.

He had told her he was a generous person, and he was, in a material sense. He could afford to be. But it could actually be argued that it wasn't generosity when the cost to him was very low. On a more emotional level, he was much more miserly. He had built thick, jaded boundaries around himself. Any respect he offered was conditional. Tentative. Everyone would disappoint him eventually. It was not a matter of if but when.

Fliss was authentically generous, though. Considering how she'd been treated in the past and then Saint's neglect of her when she'd been attacked by the press, she would have been within her rights to help him exit the plane without a parachute. It made her openness and lack of inhibition in this bed even more of a gift.

The abuse she'd suffered—and yes, it was abuse—incensed him. On top of that, he was disturbed to realize how little experience she really had with relationships. She needed more than respect. She needed to be handled with tenderness.

He didn't have a capacity for that. Inadequacy chipped at him as he recognized how *he* was likely to disappoint *her.* In his mind, the baby had been the one who needed his protection. Fliss would provide the love their child needed, and Saint would try not to be the same sort of cold bastard his own father had been. Somehow, they would rear a contributing member of society.

Fliss was more vulnerable than he'd realized, though. It was hitting him that she would need more from him than orgasms and an introduction to some top designers. She would need things he might not have within him to give.

Maybe he shouldn't marry her. He might've regarded love as a drug that wore off and left you with a horrific hangover, but she seemed to believe in it. She'd thought his parents should have divorced so they could find it.

That meant that at some point, she might expect him to let her go so she could marry someone else who—

The clench of rejection was so strong inside him, he twitched, causing her to drew a small, startled breath.

"It's okay. Go back to sleep," he whispered, securing her closer while pressing a kiss to the point of her shoulder.

She sighed and relaxed, but he lay awake a little longer, pondering that soar of feral possessiveness in him. Why? It wasn't about the baby. It wasn't even about sex.

Although sex with her was next level. And bareback sex? He would revel in that as much as she was up for. Still, as powerful as his orgasms were, that wasn't the only reason he was obsessed with her. He'd been preoccupied with her from the time he'd left her in London three months ago, thinking about her daily. He had read the gossip stories to know where she had turned up—needing to know she was alive at least. He had wanted to know if she was reading her cards and communing with her grandmother.

He had wanted to know how much of what she'd shown him of herself was real.

That was an uneasy admission. Especially because she was literally in his arms, in his bed, and he was so sexually gratified he ought to be catatonic, but there was a nagging sense of tenuousness keeping him awake.

Every relationship ran its course, whether it was a friendship or someone he hired or a liaison with a woman. He was always aware the association would end, even in the earliest stages of meeting someone new. He could see it as clearly as he saw the person he was meeting.

With Fliss, he hadn't seen the end. He hadn't had time in that initial flurry of lovemaking. Then he'd tried to force the ending, which had sat crooked inside him until he'd seen her again. He still couldn't see the day when they would part for good.

Because of the baby, obviously. Their child would keep her in his life forever, no matter what happened between them.

That was a strange, new concept. The only lifetime relationships he had were with his parents, and those were thorny as hell.

Was that why he always foresaw an end point? Because he liked walking away from people when things got difficult?

It was better than the alternative—sticking it out to stick it to the other person. Wasn't it?

Saint was still thinking about that the following day, when he left Fliss in Willow's capable hands at his New York penthouse and entered the boardroom. He was using a tablet to bring the remote board members into the meeting when his father arrived.

"You're on time at least," Ted Montgomery muttered. "Why are you doing that? Where's your assistant?"

"Good God, Dad. If I'm not capable of connecting a video chat, I have no business working here, do I?" He said into the microphone, "Can everyone hear me? Shall I start the presentation?"

"We've all seen the slides," his father dismissed. "I'm more interested in why you hared off to London. It wasn't in your schedule two days ago."

"I was rearranging some things so we can have dinner with Mother tonight."

"We?"

"It's been added to your calendar."

His father's cheek ticked. "What does she want?"

"I called it. One way or another, we'll need to debrief on what happens today." Saint was being deliberately cryptic as he held his father's challenging gaze.

On their way out of London, Saint had had a private nurse take samples for a lab. The paternity results ought to be available by the time he sat down with his parents tonight. Before he shared that news, he wanted to know where he stood at Grayscale.

"Shall we get to the vote?" he asked.

His father made an impatient noise and sat, then flicked his hand at the CFO to speak.

"Order champagne tonight," the CFO said with her warmest smile. "We wouldn't have asked you to the meeting if we weren't prepared to back you. We're particularly pleased to see how you have shifted the conversation around your personal life. This gives us the confidence that when the time comes, you'll lead Grayscale well into the future." She cut a careful glance toward Ted. "Until that time, we see the value in this new direction you're taking. I move that we support Saint's proposal."

"Second," someone murmured.

The vote was carried and the approval minuted.

"Excellent. *No backsies*, right?" Saint directed that to his father.

"I'll have Xanthe draft a press release," the CFO assured him. "It will go out this afternoon."

"Thank you." Satisfaction and a rush of pure adrenaline for the challenge washed through him. Saint had done so much preliminary work in anticipation of this, he only needed to open the gates and let the horses loose.

His usual single-mindedness was fractured, though. Weirdly, his first instinct was to call Fliss and tell her *I did it*, even though he'd only given her the bare bones of what he'd hoped to accomplish this morning. He had never been one to brag, having learned as a child that there was no point. His father took an attitude that excellence was the bare minimum. He had never been *proud* of anything his son had done.

Ted would be livid tonight, which was why Saint deliberately kept any mention of Fliss and her new place in his life to himself. It was dirty pool, but once the board's support of his project was publicized, it would be a lot harder for them to reverse course.

It would be hard for his father to reverse course once he learned about the baby, but even if it all went to hell in a handbasket...

Saint would hate that. He really would, but Fliss and the baby were his priority now—which was such a lurching departure from his usual way of thinking, he didn't know how to feel about it.

He shook hands with each of the board members, accepting their congratulations as he left them to finish their quarterly meeting.

His father only gave him a curt nod, saying dismissively, "I'll see you at dinner."

Fliss couldn't decide if she was Rapunzel, Sleeping Beauty or Cinderella.

She'd been half-asleep when they had landed and driven into the city last night. Saint had shown her around his cavernous penthouse before they'd gone back to bed, but she hadn't fully appreciated his home until she'd woken to the sunshine pouring in on her.

Situated eighty floors into the sky, it was two stories wrapped in an arc of glass offering panoramic views of the Hudson River, New York Harbor and the Statue of Liberty. She descended what looked like a glass staircase to the main floor, where a color scheme of slate and midnight blue and quiet cream welcomed her. All of his furniture was modern with rounded corners and long, flowing lines. The floors were marble and hardwood, and the area rugs were so exquisite they had to be handloomed. The contemporary abstracts on the walls were by names she didn't recognize but would look up later.

She and Saint hadn't spoken much. It had still been early, so they'd made love, eaten breakfast, showered, and then he'd dressed in a suit, telling her he had an important meeting with the board this morning. It was a special project that had been derailed by the bad publicity after their initial affair.

Fliss had grown uneasy, deducing that her presence, and pregnancy, could impact his aspirations again.

"There's still time to...not do this," she'd reminded him.

He had turned from the mirror, his tie still dangling loosely from his upturned collar, the top button of his shirt not yet closed. She'd been barefoot in her cotton pajama bottoms and a white T-shirt without a bra.

"Do you want to not do this?" His gaze had flicked to the bed they'd used with enthusiasm.

"I want to do this." She'd pointed at the floor. "Be in this room and never leave. I don't want to do that." She'd waved at the windows. "Be out there as a thing that strangers can judge."

"Good news. Your wish is granted." He'd come across to drop a kiss onto her lips that had been seductive enough that she'd leaned into it, encouraging him to linger. He'd drawn back with reluctance. "For the day, anyway. We'll have dinner with my parents tonight, but it's best if you stay inside until then. Do you mind?" He'd finished buttoning his shirt and expertly tied his tie without looking.

"Dinner? Tonight?" she'd cried. "Where? Here? Am I supposed to cook? What do I wear?"

"Wow. This is not an actual emergency. Take a breath. I've asked Willow— Ah. They're here." He'd pointed toward a muted ping that had sounded from a hidden speaker.

"Who's here? Who's Willow?"

"My executive assistant. Their pronouns are *they/them*. I'll introduce you, then I have to go. Do you mind getting dressed?" His gaze had dropped to her chest. "I like seeing your nipples through your shirt, but I'm getting possessive about who else does."

Her nipples had tightened in a responsive sting that had made her blush. He'd smirked.

She'd hurried to change while Saint had shrugged into his jacket and put on his shoes, then he'd led her down the stairs, saying, "Good morning."

"Good morning," the well-dressed twenty-something had responded. They'd worn a very smart pinstriped suit and boots with a heel. They hadn't batted an eyelash at Fliss, even though they'd known who she was because they'd said, "It's nice to meet you, Ms. Corning. I'm Willow."

"Nice to meet you, too." Fliss had shaken their hand, smiling uncertainly because even in jeans and a fresh T-shirt, *with a bra*, she'd felt very underdressed. "Please call me Fliss."

"I'll go to the office alone," Saint had said to Willow. "I need you to stay and help Fliss get settled. First order of business is to find her an obstetrician."

"Of course." Willow had drawn a phone from the inside pocket of their suit jacket, again seeming completely unfazed. "My sister has a specialist she loves. Let me ask her for the number."

"See if she has a stylist she likes, too."

"For tonight?" Fliss had asked him.

"And the foreseeable future," he'd replied, adding to Willow, "Someone stronger in procurement than opinions. Fliss knows what she wants. Make dinner reservations at that place my mother likes. Warn them that my father will be with us so they can have a steak on hand. I'll text if I think of anything else." He'd checked for his phone, then he'd dropped a kiss onto Fliss's pouted mouth. "Willow is extremely trustworthy. You're in good hands."

Seconds later, he'd been gone and she'd been alone with the stranger.

"My sister," Willow had said with a satisfied smile as their phone had pinged. "The office won't be open yet, but I'll set up a call to interview the doctor as soon as I can get through."

"Thank you. Saint ordered breakfast." Fliss had waved toward the kitchen where they had eaten at the island bar. She hadn't put it away yet. "They must have thought we were a party of thirty. There are pastries and fruit medley for days. Would you like something?"

"I've eaten, thanks, but I'll make myself a coffee." Willow had gone to the industrial grade espresso maker behind the island. "Can I make one for you, too?"

"I prefer tea, but I've had enough for now. You don't seem shocked that I'm here. Or that I…need a specialist."

"I expect the unexpected, working for Saint." Willow had reached unhesitatingly into the various cupboards, clearly familiar with the layout. "It's funny because a lot of my days are very boring. He travels and leaves me with reports to analyze, or I'm picking up dry cleaning. I start to think I'm overpaid and underutilized, then he drops a jigsaw puzzle on the table and tells me to finish it by lunch."

"Am I the jigsaw puzzle?" Fliss had guessed.

"You are. But I love puzzles," Willow had said, lips tilted with amusement.

"Me, too. I used to do them with my granny." Fliss had smiled. Maybe she didn't need to be so intimidated by Willow and their ultra-efficient manner after all.

In truth, they got along like a house on fire. The stylist, Regina, was nice, too. The only hiccup occurred when Fliss balked at ordering more than a handful of items on top of the dress she had picked out for the evening.

She was used to making her own clothing or buying from consignment and altering or embellishing to make a piece her own. There was also the fact that whatever she bought today wouldn't fit her for very long, which Willow picked up on, waiting until Regina had left to say, "Saint wants you to have everything you need for the foreseeable future. That includes maternity wear. If you're not ready to tell Regina, we can work around it, but I'm confident she could source some items without revealing who they're for."

"I'll think about it," Fliss murmured, but she really wanted to keep her pregnancy under wraps for as long as possible, certain it would put her in the spotlight again.

By the time Regina returned with three racks of clothing and a metric crap ton of shoes, it was time for Fliss to get ready. Since her prep for the gala had failed to measure up to Saint's usual crowd, she let Regina's staff do her hair and makeup and even allowed Regina to alter her dress when she would normally do that herself.

She definitely felt like Cinderella when she was pronounced "ready" and made her way out of the spare bedroom and down the stairs.

Regina had leapt on Fliss's appreciation for vintage styles with contemporary touches. She'd brought her a selection from an up-and-coming New York designer including this A-line style skirt in Mediterranean-blue satin with a black fitted bodice. It was off the shoulder while still being meet-the-parents modest. The sweetheart neckline made the most of her ample breasts while creating the illusion that she had a well-defined waist. Her shoes were a closed-toe Mary Jane with a medium heel.

Fliss felt like a screen legend from the black-and-white

era but gripped the rail with tension as she came down, half fearing that Saint's parents were here because she could hear him speaking.

He stopped mid-word when he saw her, saying into his phone, "My date is here. Forward that to my parents, and we'll talk more tomorrow."

He ended the call and came to the bottom of the stairs, trapping her on the bottom one so they were eye to eye.

She held her breath as he took in her hair, scooped into a simple twist, her red lips, her bare shoulders and cleavage, then came back up.

"So you do like my taste in earrings."

"These aren't *the* earrings?" She touched the very artistic scroll of blue-and-white stones. Regina had said they would go perfectly with her dress, so Fliss had assumed the other woman had picked them herself from some high-end costume jewelry.

"They are," he confirmed, making her stomach feel funny.

"But you're not giving them to me," she protested. "I said I didn't want any," she reminded, wondering if this meant he'd rather give her sparkly rocks than respect or regard.

"I collected them on my way to Nottingham, so I already had them when you said you didn't want them." His face blanked into the remote expression that was so hard to read. "Would you rather not accept them?"

"They're worth a fortune! It's stressful to wear things this expensive." The dress and shoes were already a lot to worry about. "Why do you want me to wear them?"

"Because you like them and they suit you?" he suggested pithily.

"It's not because…"

"What?"

"Are you trying to prove something or… I don't know," she mumbled as she saw his expression darken.

"I don't care about anyone's opinion but yours. If you like them, then I want you to have them and wear them."

"Thank you." Fliss touched her lobes to ensure each earring was secure. Her stomach was full of snakes. "I feel like you're mad at me now, and that wasn't my intention. I'm just nervous."

"I'm not mad," he said in that acerbic voice. "Not at you. I'm only realizing that the earrings will be noticed and re-marked on and that will make you self-conscious. I want you to be able to enjoy wearing a pair of damned earrings if you want to."

"What an apt description. That's what I'll call them from now one. My *damned* earrings."

Saint didn't react, only stared at her.

"Sometimes my sense of humor is misplaced," she admitted with a wrinkle of her nose.

"Now that you've found it, keep it," he drawled, helping her down the final step. "It'll help you get through dinner."

"Because they're going to hate me?" she asked with dread as they waited for the elevator.

"My father hates everyone. Don't take it personally."

"And your mother?" she asked as they stepped into the elevator.

He sighed. "Mother has always believed her looks are her only asset. Dad has never given her credit for bringing more to their marriage than beauty. As such, she despises any sign of aging. The title of grandmother will be a knife to her heart."

"Do we have to do this in public?" she asked as they exited and stepped into the waiting car.

"We do," he said firmly.

The drive wasn't far. The restaurant was smallish, obviously very exclusive given the way they were escorted from the curb up carpeted steps that were protected by a black awning lit by fairy lights. They were handed off to a middle-aged maître d' who had the air of someone who had made a career out of this work.

"Mr. Montgomery. Welcome. I just seated your parents. Please follow me."

Saint had taken hold of Fliss's hand as they'd left the car. He had to feel how clammy her palm was, but he forged the way, allowing her to trail behind him as they wound through the full tables. She tried not to crane her neck, even though she recognized a few celebrities. It was disconcerting to realize they were looking back, noticing Saint and maybe recognizing her from her photos.

She tried to focus on the clothes as a distraction, and it worked a little too well. She nearly crashed into Saint when he stopped walking. He steadied her as he brought her to stand beside him.

"Mom. Dad. I'd like you to meet Felicity."

Fliss's anxiety turned to the sort of morbid terror that came from facing something she knew wasn't genuinely life-threatening but still turned her blood cold, like a giant spider.

The couple stole a moment to recover from their shock, then rose politely. Ted Montgomery was a peek at what

Saint would look like in forty years—distinguished and even more stern, still wearing an aura of power that hadn't diminished at all.

His mother was the source of his star power, though. Norma was easily fifteen years younger than her husband. Her figure was fit, not the least bit matronly. She wore a sequined drop-waist dress that glinted and shimmered in the candlelight. Her beauty would have been a standard blonde-and-blue-eyed variety if not for an intrinsic sparkle that might have dimmed with age, but it was still there, demanding she be noticed.

"How charming. Call me Norma," his mother said, offering her hand in a very brief, weak shake. Her cool gaze skimmed down, taking in every detail of Fliss's appearance, including coming back to the earrings before transferring a silent question toward Saint.

"Ted." His father didn't offer to shake hands. He moved to help Norma with her chair.

"A bottle of Dom," Saint said to the hovering maître d' as he held Fliss's chair.

She sank gratefully into it, knees weak. Her throat had constricted so tightly she felt as though she sipped oxygen through a straw.

"This is why you went to London?" Ted asked with only a flickering glance toward Fliss before shifting his glare back to his son. "You didn't say a word about her in our meeting this morning."

"I was waiting on an email that I've forwarded to both of you," Saint said blithely. "You can read it later, but the important piece is that you're being informed of our happy news at the same time. I'm not playing favorites."

"Hap— Saint." His mother's voice was a gust of betrayal.

"There's no dispute?" His father reached for his phone.

"None," Saint assured him. "I sent it to Elijah so he can begin making adjustments to my will."

Ted sent her a look that was both accusation and disgust. His mother's eyes gleamed with angry tears.

"Wow," Fliss couldn't help saying. "When you said your family dinners were a nightmare, you meant it."

Shock slacked everyone's jaws.

"Oh, did I say that out loud?" She facetiously touched her lips. "I thought that's what we were doing."

Ted's gaze narrowed. Norma's gaze dropped, and her red face turned redder.

Saint sat back, angling to face her.

She'd gone too far, she knew she had, but she had her passport in her clutch and enough room on her credit card to get herself back to London. She could go straight to the airport from here. She didn't have to put up with anyone treating her this way.

"As I said, I'd like you to meet Felicity," Saint drawled. A glimmer of admiration stole into his expression as he continued looking at her. "How you feel about her is irrelevant. How you treat her is not." He sat straight again, making a point of looking at both of his parents in turn. "If you drive her away, you drive me away, so think about the words that are coming out of your mouths."

The bucket of champagne arrived with four crystal flutes.

Saint held up a finger to hit pause on the popping of the cork.

"Are we staying?" he asked them.

CHAPTER NINE

SAINT WOKE AT four in the morning to find the bed beside him empty. The sheets were cool. He lurched up in bed.

"Fliss?"

She wasn't in the bathroom. The door was open, the room dark.

He shrugged on his robe and padded downstairs, finding her in a pool of lamplight, kneeling at the coffee table. A cup of tea was steaming near her elbow. On the table in front of her were three cards face up on a square of black velvet.

"Do you always do this during the witching hour?"

"My body is still on London time. I couldn't sleep." She sipped her tea. "I decided to see what I could see."

"And what do you see?" He started to lower into the chair opposite her.

"That's Granny's spot." She pointed at the cup of milky brown tea on the side table, also releasing a wisp of steam.

"Excuse me, Granny," he said to the empty chair, nonplussed, and moved to sit behind Fliss so he could peer over her shoulder. Three cards were laid in a row. The image in the middle was right side up, but the ones on the outside were upside down.

"The Empress is abundance." Fliss touched the card on the left. "And love. Venus." She pointed to a symbol. "She's reversed because the abundance I'm enjoying is yours, not mine. And because my love is flowing out." She nodded at the empty chair. "Not back to me."

Saint was skeptical of all of this, but he couldn't be dismissive. Her profile was too solemn. She'd been through a lot in the last thirty-six hours or so. If she needed to pretend her grandmother was here so she didn't feel so alone, who was he to judge?

He gave her silky hair a pet and left his hand on her shoulder.

"What about your pregnancy? Venus is the goddess of fertility, isn't she?" He leaned forward to lift the Empress onto its top edge. "Aren't babies usually upside down inside the womb? Maybe that's what it means."

She twisted a glare of mock horror at him and whispered, "Don't touch my cards." She delicately took it to lay it down again. "But thank you. I like that interpretation."

"What's the stick?" He pointed to the one in the middle, labeled *Ace of Wands*.

"That's your fault."

"Oh?"

"It's a new idea that is starting to take root in my mind. You said I should focus on lingerie, and I can't stop thinking about that. It's really hard—"

"The stick?"

"Lingerie." She slid him another admonishing look.

"But you can see from the way that fist is clutching that very sturdy branch, I thought the interpretation was going in a different direction."

"And you can see that the cards never lie. You see what you want to see."

Saint wanted to see her smile. She hadn't since before dinner, but at least her tone had lightened.

"For the record, my lingerie remark was not serious when I made it." He gathered her hair as he spoke so he was holding the thick rope of it in his stacked fists. He carefully dragged her head back to see her face. "But I wholeheartedly support your shift in focus. In fact, I'll volunteer to be your beta tester."

"You want to wear one of my G-strings to see if it's comfortable?"

"You're a brat sometimes, aren't you?"

"I'm not the one barging in on a reading, pulling hair and making jokes about your penis."

"I never joke about my penis." He released her hair.

"Stick with me, kid," she murmured, straightening the Ace of Wands.

He chuckled and caged her with his knees, massaging her shoulders. "What's with the naked woman and the watering cans?"

"The Star follows the Tower in the Major Arcana. I had the Tower when I realized I was pregnant, so it makes sense that the Star has turned up." She touched the card so it was perfectly aligned with the others. "It's a symbol of hope, like a wishing star or a guiding star. She's watering the seeds that she's planted, but she's naked so she's vulnerable, which we always are when we hope."

"But it's upside down."

"I know," Fliss said pensively. "Reversed means a lack of faith or a likely disappointment. Granny always points out that *star* spelled backwards is *rats*." She tapped the word on the bottom of the card.

"Is she really here? Because there goes my plan to seduce you on the couch." He looked to the empty chair and the untouched cup of tea. "Come back to bed. I promise you won't be disappointed."

She only picked up her tea to sip. "That was a really difficult dinner, Saint."

He knew. That was why he'd been genuinely alarmed to find the bed empty and so relieved to find her here. His parents had stayed and they hadn't said anything that was outright antagonistic or insulting, but they hadn't welcomed her with open arms. Aside from his mother asking about her due date, they'd barely acknowledged the baby.

"And this Belmont Stakes thing? I don't know anything about horses!"

"Is that the reason you couldn't sleep?" he asked.

"It's a house party for a *week*," she said. "Why didn't you warn me?"

"I forgot about it, or I would have. Mom actually has a horse in the race this year. That's not an expression—she really does. So we can't refuse to go." The timing was terrible, though, with his project still in such early stages of getting off the ground. "It's an excellent chance for me to introduce you to everyone, though."

"Who is 'everyone'?"

"Mom's horsey friends." And the Hampton circle along with his father's cronies and the board members who would be sucking lemons over the sleight of hand Saint had pulled by failing to mention Fliss when he had accepted their backing. "Don't worry. It's a week away."

"I looked it up, Saint," she said. "I need outfits. I need *hats*. Your mother was already looking at me like I was an embarrassment."

"I told you, she's vain about her age. She'll come around."

"I always hoped my baby would have a grandmother like I did," she admitted softly.

His gaze flickered to that upside-down Star of disappointment.

"I would give that to you if I could, Fliss." He leaned forward to cup the front of her throat and press a kiss to the top of her hair. "I want to give you everything you need. I really do." When it came to his parents, a sense of failure, of being robbed was so visceral, it was bitter on his tongue.

He did what he always did when emotions reared their head.

"Let's talk to a Realtor tomorrow to find a space for your design work."

"I'd rather use one of the spare bedrooms. I only need a table for my sewing machine, and I'd rather not go out every day and have to worry about being photographed." She began gathering up her cards, then paused. "Do you want me to do a reading for you?"

"God, no." Saint cleared his throat. "I mean, no, thank you."

"Chicken. What are you afraid I'll see?" She was finally smiling as she folded the velvet around the cards and secured the package with a white ribbon.

Too much. The answer slithered through his mind, too slippery to catch and examine, but it was true.

* * *

They flew by helicopter, landing in a private airfield where they were collected by a chauffeur who greeted Saint with warm familiarity and a welcoming smile for Fliss.

His mother was less effusive when they arrived at the end of a secluded driveway in a cobbled courtyard surrounding a fountain before a massive stone mansion with wings off either side. It was topped with gingerbread detailing and a tile roof.

Norma greeted them with perfunctory cheek kisses and directed their luggage to "the junior suite."

"I'll leave you to show Felicity around. The florist finally arrived, and they brought the wrong color lilies so I have that disaster on my hands." She stalked away.

"Oh no," Saint said faintly in her wake.

"She just wants her party to go well," Fliss murmured, but if the wrong lilies were a disaster, what did that make her?

During that awful dinner last week, she'd been politely interrogated on her life, from her upbringing to her education right up to her aspiration to pursue fashion design. At no point had she felt that Mr. and Mrs. Montgomery had warmed to her.

As Saint showed her around, Fliss's apprehension grew. His penthouse was gorgeous and worth millions, but this was only *one* of his parents' residences. His father stayed in their Fifth Avenue apartment while Norma spent most of her time at their twenty-two-acre estate in Bedford Corners. They called this mansion their "cottage."

It had been built for entertaining. The main floor was open and welcoming with a great room containing a massive fireplace, a number of smaller conversation areas and a formal dining room with seating for sixteen. Every room had windows and doors onto the back garden where a huge patio was surrounded by flowering shrubs and June blooms.

Saint pointed out the games room and home movie theatre—it easily sat twenty.

"The fitness room and sauna are below our suite in the other wing. I'll show you on the way to our room." He walked her outside past the enormous kidney-shaped pool. "I wanted us to have the pool house, but that's the beauty salon this week. If you chip a nail or want your hair done, just come here. Do you play tennis?" He nodded to the court that was tucked into the trees at the end of a short path.

"Never." She was still craning her neck back at the pool house, which was a genuine cottage with a chimney, a porch, hanging baskets and rickrack detailing.

They stepped onto a boardwalk that wound through grassy sand dunes, then descended onto the longest, emptiest beach Fliss had ever seen. The ocean stretched out in a gray-blue rippling blanket for about a thousand miles.

"Is that England I see over there?" she joked, pointing randomly.

"That's West Africa." Saint took hold of her shoulders and angled her so she was looking almost straight up the beach. "Northeast is that way, but Canada's elbow is in the way."

"Oh, Canada," she groused. "Can't you see I'm homesick?"

"Are you?" His arms came around her, drawing her back into his strong frame. "I thought you were settling in."

"I am," she fibbed because he could be so sweet sometimes, holding her like this. She draped her arms over his as they watched the waves rolling onto the sand.

At least she had her studio in the penthouse to make her feel at home. It was so much her dream workspace she nearly cried with joy every time she entered it. But the time she spent in there was less about pursuing her dream and more about escaping the reality of this new, foreign life she'd been thrust into.

Her other escape was, of course, this. His arms. The feel of him nuzzling into her neck and thickening against her backside sent tingles showering from her scalp into her breasts. Tendrils of warmth wound into her pelvis whenever he so much as glanced at her. None of her worries could impact her when they spent their nights—and mornings and stolen midday moments—kissing and fondling and pleasuring each other into oblivion.

They cushioned the culture shock of what she was going through, but none of it changed the fact that she felt as though she'd won an all-expenses-paid vacation and was enjoying a holiday fling.

How could she settle into a life that wasn't real?

"Why don't I show you where we'll be sleeping?" Saint suggested throatily.

"You're losing your touch," she teased, reaching back to comb her fingers into his silky hair. "I'm surprised you haven't shown me already."

"The maid needed time to unpack your *six* suitcases." He was also teasing, but all Fliss could think was that they weren't her cases. They might've been rose pink where his were black, but they'd been purchased by him and contained clothing he had bought. She'd approved the outfits after being coached on the robust itinerary of appearances and events and the expected dress code for each. One whole case was dedicated to lotions and cosmetics and hair products.

Hand in hand, they climbed the steps back onto the boardwalk. The house came into view in all its dramatic glory, wings reaching out like arms to cradle the glimmering pool.

"This is really beautiful." She paused, absorbing that this property, along with all those other ones she hadn't yet seen, would be his one day.

"I prefer my beach house in California."

She swallowed a semi-hysterical laugh and let him lead her back to the house, then up some stairs to a massive suite decorated in powder blue and silvery white. Fliss took a moment to wander the sitting room with its small dining nook, then peeked onto the balcony with its view of the ocean. The sumptuous bathroom held a claw-footed tub and a shower that could have doubled as a parking garage. The bed was as big as the pool.

Saint came toward her from checking that both doors to the hall were locked, toeing off his shoes along the way, releasing the buttons at his throat as he did.

Her mouth went dry, always. He was so deliberate yet casual in his sexuality.

"This is the junior suite?" she said with a weak smile.

"The main one has separate bedrooms. Not something we'll ever need, hmm?" He used the back of one crooked finger to caress the edge of her jaw.

Fliss had known he was rich, but this was…impossible. *They* were impossible.

"What's wrong?" He tilted her chin up and frowned as he searched her gaze.

She was drowning. Suffocating.

"Nothing," she lied, offering her lips.

Because, when he covered them, she melted into that different reality where she belonged right here, pressed up against him so tightly she imagined she could feel his chest hairs through the fabric of their shirts.

She was growing bolder, learning what he liked, and slid her hand to the front of his trousers to squeeze him.

Saint grunted and backed her toward the bed, tugging at her clothing as he did.

Moments later, they were naked on the sheets, covers thrown back, kissing passionately. "Be inside me," she urged, finding the bold, aroused length that brushed her inner thigh. She guided him to her center. "I need to feel you."

"Careful," he murmured, caressing her briefly before taking control and sliding the damp tip of his erection against her sensitive inner lips. "You're not ready yet. Why the rush? We have two hours before we're expected to make an appearance."

"I know, but..." Everything would change in a few hours. The gossip sites had cottoned on to their relationship. They'd been photographed going out to dinner and shopping, but now they would be scrutinized up close by his peers—she would.

"Let me make it good for you." He began running his hands over her body as though learning her anew, until every skin cell was awakened to his touch. Then he followed with the lazy graze of his lips. Damp kisses made flames of yearning lick through her so she was aching with need by the time he tipped her thighs back and settled his mouth against her most sensitive flesh.

When she was quivering with tension and on the point of breaking, he rose over her. Now he surged into her the way she needed. She had the taste of herself on her tongue as he sealed his lips to hers in a ravishing kiss. The first ripples of climax had her moaning into his mouth, twisting in the agony of supreme pleasure. He held her in that state with his superior strength and the slow, powerful plunge of his sex into hers.

This was where she needed to be, encased in the electric excitement of raw lovemaking, connected to him in a way that transcended the physical.

Now she only needed to touch his shoulder and he knew what she wanted. He rolled onto his back, and she sat up to ride the rhythm he set. She pinched his nipple and played her fingers over where they joined, knowing he liked it.

Saint's lips peeled back, baring his teeth as he fought to hold on to his control. His cheeks were flushed dark with lust. His fingertips would leave bruises where he gripped her hips, matching the ones fading from last night or the time before that.

When the intensity grew too much for her and she closed her eyes and let her head fall back, succumbing to her thunderous orgasm, he arched beneath her, lifting her off the bed as he shouted with his own release.

Fliss slumped weakly upon him in the aftermath, loving the descent almost as much as the pinnacle. She liked feeling his heart pounding against her breast and hearing the rattle of his breath and knowing she'd done that to him.

She liked the twitch of him still inside her, slowly relaxing. She liked the lazy way his hands petted her back in such a tender way.

"See?" he murmured. "We even have time for a nap."

She carefully extricated herself from him and drew the sheet up so it fell between them, forming a small barrier because she had realized what was really bothering her.

People were going to look at her and see not just that she lacked an Ivy League education and wasn't rich and famous and couldn't tell a thoroughbred from a pack mule. She could stand that. She didn't care about them enough to care what they thought of her.

But they would see that this was all she had with Saint. Sex. They hadn't known each other long enough to even form something that could be called a true friendship, let alone the warmer connection of real lovers.

Actually, it wasn't even that other people would guess how little she meant to him. It was her. She was realizing that even though he was considerate and generous and gave her such high-voltage orgasms they could power a small country, he didn't really care about her. Not any more than he would about Willow or a stray kitten they found on the beach. He would look after her and be kind to her, but he wouldn't give her his heart.

And that hurt.

Because there wasn't a damned thing she could do about it.

CHAPTER TEN

"The Belton-Websters are some of my parents' oldest friends," Saint told Fliss two days later, when an older man sent a friendly salute of his rolled program from another box at the track. Saint tipped his straw boater hat in reply. "Walter is on the board at Grayscale. They have a home in Water Mill. I was at Harvard with their eldest son, Kyle. If we don't see them at lunch, we'll meet them tonight at their party."

They were in the shade, but it was hot enough that Saint wanted to unbutton the cream-colored vest he wore with matching trousers over a pale blue shirt and a navy bowtie.

The clubhouse lounge, which his mother bought out every year as a giant flex, was air-conditioned and had an open bar along with the buffet she provided to her carefully curated guest list. It wasn't enough to have an owner's box, where a server brought them drinks and snacks on demand and they had a front-row seat to the finish line along with the entertainment between races. He and Fliss also had it to themselves. Norma was currently down at the paddock. Saint's father wouldn't turn up until the big race tomorrow.

"That will be nice," Fliss said with a blank smile, feigning enthusiasm.

He'd been introducing her to people nonstop, first at dinner, then a cocktail party appearance, brunch yesterday, an afternoon garden party and another soiree last night. This was all very rote to him, the faces all slotted into their pigeonholes of usefulness.

Fliss was holding up well. Today she wore yet another perfectly on-point outfit that was sufficiently demure to meet the expected dress code but was also flattering enough to stop traffic. Her pink-and-green floral lace dress hugged her figure and fell to her knees in front, draping longer in the back. The sleeves flared at her elbow, and the neckline plunged enough to make the most of her spectacular chest, which Saint had adorned with a vintage gold necklace he'd chosen for its horseshoe charm. Rather than a hat, she wore her hair in a tight bun wrapped in a pink band. A pair of cats-eye sunglasses and bold fuchsia lipstick completed the look.

Despite the sophistication she projected, she was tense, struggling to smile at each new face. Sometimes he caught her stifling a yawn.

"Dad had an affair with Mrs. Belton-Webster," he said, leaning closer to confide.

Fliss swung her head around and tipped her sunglasses down to look over them, eyes glimmering with shock.

That woke her up. Saint shrugged.

"They don't know I know. I figured out that Mom knew about it when they didn't show up to their daughter's wedding. It's all water under the bridge now. I think one of the reasons Mom stayed with Dad was because she was more afraid of losing that friendship than him. Or her place in all of this." He used his chin to gesture to the racetrack. "You'll keep all of that to yourself."

"Of course." She sipped the straw of her mint-julep mocktail. "Why did you tell me if you thought I would repeat it?"

"You seemed bored." And he'd never had a confidante to tell. He'd had to let things like that fester inside himself, trying to work out what to do, how to react and when to let it go because his parents had.

"I'm not bored. I've just given up on trying to keep it all straight. I mean, I can't get to know every person *and* every horse. You seem to have friends everywhere, though. You came here often growing up? I don't mean the track. The beach house."

"We came here in the summer if we were living in the city, but we lived in Texas and California at different times. I felt like a military brat, making friends, then leaving for a few years, adjusting to a new situation, then coming back and trying to fit in with the old crowd." Eventually, he'd grown tired of trying. "I do know a lot of people. I don't consider any of them friends."

Her liquid-honey gaze searched his, making his chest itch.

The bell rang.

"Oh!" Fliss swung her attention to the track. "They're off."

At least she was having fun with the betting. She'd been appalled when he had told her he would stake her ten grand. He had threatened to pick her horses himself if she didn't spend it, so she had sat down with the program and her tarot cards, making her selections before they'd even arrived to glimpse the horses.

She'd won the first race, but her bet had been so small, she'd only come away with eight hundred dollars, which she'd tried to give to him.

"Double down," he had insisted, so he knew she had at least that much riding on this race. He'd dropped five grand, and things were not looking good.

"Which one is yours?" he asked.

Fliss's hand came out to grasp his arm. Otherwise, she wasn't moving, wasn't breathing. She was transfixed by the sprinting horses.

"The one in front?" he guessed, starting to grin as her expression began to glow.

"Shh." Her grip crushed his sleeve.

It was like watching her as she approached climax. Her breath was uneven. Her breasts trembled. Anticipation radiated off her, tightening his own nerves.

It was titillating enough to set hooks into Saint's libido, but he was also amused in a completely non-carnal way. She was mesmerizing, looking so sexy and cutely rapt at the same time. He was twitching into arousal and wanting this win for her in a way he'd never wanted anything, just so he could see her reaction.

If the race had gone one second longer, he would have been fully hard, but there was a collective roar. Fliss screamed in triumph and leapt into his arms, crashing her curves against him, filling his senses with floral and citrus notes that he was learning were innately her. She was warm and soft beneath the thin layer of crepe, light and lovely. Her wild excitement provoked a rusty scrape of laughter in his throat, one that stalled when he noticed his father had turned up after all. He was watching them.

Saint's first, most primal instinct was to draw her protectively closer, but another more harshly learned response recognized that he had revealed a weakness.

He set her back a step. "How much did you win?"

"Enough to pay you back your stake." She was jubilant, smile wide and eyes bright as she straightened the sunglasses that had been knocked askew.

"I don't want it back. It's for you to play all weekend," he reminded.

She did pay him back, though, since she had doubled her money by the end of the day.

"Beginner's luck," she claimed that evening when they were on the terrace at the Belton-Websters'. Word had got around that Fliss had been on a hot streak today. Everyone wanted to know her secret. "Also my lucky horseshoe." She picked up the pendant she wore.

"Have you looked at tomorrow's races?" a middle-aged man asked her.

"I'm saving most of my money for Paprika's Tuft," she said, mentioning Norma's thoroughbred. "But there are a couple others that look promising."

"Show me." The man had his program and a pencil in hand.

Saint excused himself to the bar and was returning with a fresh drink when he ran into Kyle, the son of their host that he'd told Fliss about. Kyle was newly divorced and a little drunker than was wise.

"So that's her, the one who got you in trouble with Dad and the rest of the board?" Kyle snickered, his attention twisted to where Fliss still had her head together with the older man. "I see the attraction. *Nice.*" His hand came up to his chest, cupping imaginary breasts.

"That's your one shot, Kyle. Leave it there, and I'll forget we had this conversation." It was a lie. Saint would never forget. He wanted to blacken both his eyes.

"She's a *housemaid.* You're not serious about her," Kyle scoffed. "Let me know when you're done with her, though."

"We're getting married." Saint squared himself against the man, planting his feet. "She's going to be the mother of my child." He blindly reached to the table beside him to set down his drink.

He missed. The smash of glass on the stones silenced the din of conversation, but Saint didn't look anywhere but at Kyle's disbelieving smirk.

"Swallow what you just said, or I'll shove those words back down your throat for you," Saint warned.

"She's *pregnant*?" Kyle guffawed into the silence. "Man, I gave you a lot more credit than you deserved."

The heel of Saint's palm hit the middle of Kyle's chest before he realized that he was reacting. It was a shove, not a strike, but it was strong enough to send Kyle stumbling backward. His arms flailed as he hit the edge of the pool, then he was plummeting backward into it. The splash washed across nearby shoes, making everyone gasp and step back.

"Saint!" His mother's voice cut through the murmur of shock.

Kyle was slapping at the water, clumsily swimming to the edge, swearing a blue streak.

Saint resisted the urge to stand on the man's head. He

looked for Fliss and found her staring at him with the same appalled shock as everyone else.

All heads turned to her now, making her the center of attention as everyone reevaluated her dress, which was three long layers of pleated ruffles from a single shoulder strap, disguising her thickening waistline.

"She *does* bet on the right horse, doesn't she?" an amused voice gurgled.

"Shut up," Saint said in the direction of the voice.

Fliss pivoted on one sandal and walked into the house.

"Fliss!" Saint caught up to her in the music room.

Fliss was so furious she couldn't even look at him. "I need the ladies' room."

"You're not locking yourself in a bathroom," he said through his teeth, looming closer.

"I *will* use the loo when I need one!" She paused long enough to glare a warning at him. "Take away every other bloody right I have, but not that one."

Heads swiveled in their direction, the level of acute curiosity sizzling on the air like electricity building for a lightning strike.

"It's this way," he said tightly and directed her through an archway and into a short corridor.

Tempted as she was to crawl out the window, she flushed and washed her hands and came out a few minutes later.

Saint was leaning on the wall, arms folded, expression grim. He straightened. "The car is waiting outside."

"Oh, are we leaving?" she asked with facetious surprise.

"You want to stay?" He held her simmering gaze without flinching.

"Does it matter what I want?" She stalked ahead of him to the door.

He waited until they were in the back of the car to say belligerently, "I didn't like what he said."

"I didn't like what *you* said. Can I push you in the pool?"

"Will it get us over this spat as quickly as possible?"

"Is that what this is? Tell me I'm overreacting, Saint. *I dare you.*"

He waited a beat, then spoke in an ultra-calm voice that was so condescending, she wanted to hit him. "The news was going to come out eventually."

"I asked you for one thing." Fliss's voice shook despite her best efforts to keep it level. She removed her necklace and earrings and dropped them into the cup holder that was closest to him in the console between them. For good measure, she toed off her shoes and pushed them toward him with her foot.

"Really? You're going to go barefoot to prove a point? It was his disrespect toward you that got under my skin." Saint was speaking through his teeth again. "Now they know where you stand in my estimation."

"Do they?" she cried. "You have no idea how hard this is for me, do you? That I have to use *your* money to pretend I belong here when I absolutely do not and everyone knows it? They see straight through me, but I soldier on, pretending for your sake that I can't tell they can barely bring themselves to speak to me. *I'm* trying not to embarrass *you.* And I keep telling myself that it's okay that you don't know how hard this all is because you *can't* know. You've never been in this situation. So I accept your ignorance."

He opened his mouth, and she held up a finger.

"It's the part where you don't *care* how hard this is for me—and just went ahead and made it harder—that I can't forgive. Yes, I know exactly where I stand in your estimation, Saint. Guess where you stand in mine?"

They didn't speak again until they were back in their suite, but all Fliss said was, "I'm going to bed." She removed her makeup and did just that.

She was so tired she fell into a deep sleep immediately, but after a few hours, her turmoil of emotions conjured an old dream that was nightmare and memory combined. Granny was gathering her into her arms, speaking before she'd fully awaked.

I'm sorry, pet. I'm so sorry. At least you were safe here with me and not in the car with them.

"Fliss, wake up." Saint's voice was a hard snap that had her gasping and fighting the blankets and his arms, trying to sit up. "Are you okay?" His hand slid across her back as he gathered her closer, but she pushed away from him, heart pounding, skin clammy.

"Don't." She realized her cheeks were wet and reached to the nightstand for a tissue.

"Was it just a nightmare or…?"

Just? All of this was a nightmare!

She grabbed her pillow and swung it around, managing to catch him by surprise enough that he took a face full of silk and feathers before he cursed and grabbed the pillow, throwing it off the bed.

"You sounded like you were in pain," he said with fresh frustration. "Tell me you're okay. Is the baby okay?"

"The baby is fine. *I* am not okay. I thought I could count on you a *little*. But all you did was tell everyone the only reason you're keeping me around is because your previous lover sabotaged your birth control."

"I did not say that. *No one* knows that part of it."

"*I* know it!" And recalling that particular detail provoked a fresh sense of abandonment that was so acute she could hardly bear it.

Fliss rose and went into the bathroom for a robe, tying it over the pajamas she wore.

"Where are you going?" he asked as she ghosted through the dim room toward the sitting area.

"I want some tea."

"I'll phone for some."

"Oh, my *gawd*. This maid is already up." She slid the belt of the robe higher on her waist so it was more comfortable. "There's no use waking another to boil a kettle." She resisted the urge to slam the door on her way out.

By the time she was filling the kettle in the kitchen— which was such a beautiful space of cornflower blue and daffodil yellow it shouldn't even be cooked in—Saint was arriving.

She pretended to ignore him, but how could she when his white T-shirt hugged his shoulders and chest and his pajama bottoms lovingly draped the firm muscles of his buttocks? How dare he be so mouthwatering and such a complete toad at the same time?

Since she'd already had her daily allotment of black tea, she searched out the peppermint and dropped a bag into a cup while she waited for the kettle.

He clicked the button to warm the griddle, then opened the fridge to take out cheddar cheese. He buttered two slices of sour dough, then set them face down on the griddle, topped them with cheese, then topped each with another slice of bread, butter side up.

"I didn't know you were a chef," she said with only a hint of sarcasm.

"Grilled cheese, eggs and I can stick a banana in a bowl of ice cream and call it a sundae."

"If you plan to cook that sundae, I have notes. Do you want tea?" she asked as the kettle started to whistle.

He shook his head and stayed at the stove while she sat down at the island with her cup. She wasn't hungry—or any less mad at him—but she was fascinated enough by his economical movements to watch him fry a sandwich. He plated them, cut them in half, then added a blob of ketchup to each plate before sliding one toward her.

"I am on your side, Fliss," he said as he took the chair next to her. "You can count on me."

She winced, pained at how much she wanted to believe that but just couldn't.

"You can," he insisted.

"Don't sound so insulted," she mumbled, blowing across the cup she cradled in her cold hands. "Life happens. I should have been able to rely on my parents, but they were struck by a drunk driver on a blind corner."

And were gone. Just *gone*. Then she'd moved in with Granny, which meant the friends she'd had at school were also gone. Making new ones had felt impossible when she'd been so sad. As a teen, she'd finally gotten in with an in-crowd—who had turned her out after her breakup with her puerile knob of a boyfriend. Then Granny had gotten so sick and died on her, and even her loose friendships in London had evaporated after her scandal.

Counting on people had been stamped out of her DNA. She had herself. That was the only person she really believed in and, honestly, she made some pretty stupid decisions sometimes, too.

"I've already started the paperwork to ensure you'll be taken care of, should anything happen to me," Saint said gravely. "Dad has accepted that the baby is mine. Our child will inherit everything that is coming to me. You'll always have access to whatever you need, Fliss."

"This is not about money, Saint." She set down her cup. "Granny was right there, holding me when she told me my parents were dead. I still felt abandoned. That's why I wanted to do this on my own. So I wouldn't count on you, then wind up disappointed."

His cough-curse sounded as though it had been punched out of him.

"*You're* self-sufficient," she pointed you. "Why do you begrudge me wanting that for myself? Instead you want me to rely on you. You made me come live with you and become dependent on you, then you threw away my trust like it doesn't even matter."

"I brought you here because I want you here," he insisted.

"For the baby, I know," she said on a sigh that was more a sob of anguish. "I can see how important it is that our baby grows up like this so they don't feel like I do—as though they're visiting another planet. I'm trying to adapt, Saint, I really am. And I'm trying to keep my expectations low where you're concerned. I don't expect you to love me. I don't expect anything from you except—" She cut herself off.

"What?" he prompted.

"Nothing," she decided, pushing her plate away. "I thought I could expect…kindness? Regard? But I have to find those things in myself. I know that." Why was life so bloody lonely? "I'm going back to bed."

"Did you hear what I just said?" His gritted voice stopped her. "I brought you here because I want *you* here."

"For sex, yes. I know." She turned and put out a pleading hand. "Don't make it sound like more than it is. That's not fair to me."

"It's the truth, Fliss. Yes, I brought you here because of the baby, but the baby isn't even real to me yet. It's a concept. I feel…protective, I guess? I'm anxious for a positive outcome and bothered that I have so little control over that. Mostly it's a gray fog that I don't know how to navigate, so I'm not even thinking about it. I had options, though. I could have arranged protection for you or did as you asked and claimed the baby wasn't mine. I could have worked out a custody arrangement and hired a nanny to cover my side of it. God knows I know what constitutes a good one of those, having been raised by them myself. I didn't want to do any of those things. I wanted *you* here."

"For se—"

"For more than sex," he near-shouted, rising off his stool.

"Keep your voice down," she hissed, hugging herself and looking to the ceiling.

"Yes, I want to have sex with you. You're in the same bed with me. You know it's amazing. That's why you want it, too. But it's more than that, Fliss." He pushed his hair off his forehead and left his hand on his head as though trying to keep the top of his skull from popping off. "You're damned right I want you to rely on me. I don't know what else to give you. And I don't know how to deal with someone who doesn't want *things*. Who only cares if she's under a dry roof, not how big it is or which neighborhood it's located in."

Fliss bit her lips because they felt so unsteady and searched his tortured expression, wary of believing him because she really, really didn't want to be disappointed in him again, but she could tell how much this was costing him to admit.

"You got under my skin from the second I saw you. I call it lust because if I call it something else, it feels dangerous," he admitted gruffly. "It means that a drunk I see once every three years can say something about you that makes me act like a Neanderthal. You think I behave that way every day?" He waved his hand in a vague direction. "Never. When I say people know how I feel about you now, I mean they know they can get to me through you. It's terrifying."

She didn't want to be moved in any way by that, but she was. A little. She crushed the sleeve of her robe in her fist, emotions crashing around in her chest like storm waves.

"Do you see how insulting that is, though?" she asked. "That you don't want to care about me? That you resent that you do?"

"You don't want to care about me," Saint shot back, stabbing the air between them with his finger. "You don't trust me. You don't want to rely on me. You're only here for the baby. You think I don't know you have an exit strategy? If you search for train tickets to Toronto, where Mrs. Bhamra's sister lives, I'm going to get ads for them in my feed. How the hell am I supposed to trust *you* when you keep one foot out the door?"

"She's talking about visiting," Fliss mumbled, looking down at the elegant arcs of gold painted against her cuticles on her otherwise pink nails.

"I shouldn't have blurted out that you're pregnant. I know that," he said begrudgingly. "You're right that people haven't been taking you seriously. That's on me. I have a history of not taking any of my relationships seriously. But I said it so Kyle would know this is different. Now everyone knows this is different. And yes, maybe it was also a move to lock you in. Not consciously, but… I don't know." He ran his hand over his face. "I want you here, Fliss. You. And I hate myself for hurting you. I'm sorry."

Oh, what was she supposed to do now? Her anger was washing away like footprints in sand, leaving her feeling more vulnerable than ever.

"Can we at least not be angry anymore?" He held out a hand.

"What do *you* have to be angry about?" she grumbled as she stepped close enough to let him draw her into his arms.

"You clocked me with a pillow, for starters." He hugged her securely. "Disparaged my cooking skills. Accused me of human rights violations."

"Pregnant women need the loo. And I was moving the pillow. It's not my fault your face got in the way."

"My mistake. See? I'm getting the hang of relationships."

She hummed a small laugh as she tucked her face against his chest, wanting to stay in this moment of reconciliation forever. But.

"We have to go to the track tomorrow, don't we?" she said with dread.

"No," he said firmly, dropping his arms away from her. "I've already told my pilot we're flying back to the city first thing."

"Saint. Your mom will be devastated if we don't watch the race. If her horse doesn't win, who will console her? Your dad? It will be awkward for me, I know, but it won't get less awkward if I put it off, so let's get it over with."

"You think Paprika's Tuft won't win?" he asked with a frown. "What did your cards say?"

"I don't ask questions I don't want the answer to."

He narrowed his eyes. "What do your cards say about us?"

"I haven't asked."

CHAPTER ELEVEN

PAPRIKA'S TUFT LOST by a nose. Norma was disappointed but mollified by the quarter of a million dollars that was the second-prize purse.

Fliss had another good day with two wins and a shrewd win-place-show cover of bets in the final race. Her biggest return came when the man who had shadowed her bets gave her his business card.

"Call my assistant the next time you're on your way to Paris. She'll have accounts opened at whichever boutiques you like to visit."

"Oh, that's kind of you, but I couldn't." She looked to Saint, nonplussed.

"I'm up four hundred thousand dollars today. You ought to have a cut of those winnings," the man insisted.

"Take the card," Saint said mildly. "Send him your business plan. See if he'd like to bet on *you*. Fliss designs lingerie," he told the man.

"Ah. Yes. I'd like to see that proposal."

His immediate interest plucked against her sense of not working hard enough to earn such an advantage, but it was a nice outcome to end what had been a tense day. She'd been braced for the worst, but it hasn't been as uncomfortable as

Fliss had feared. There'd been too much action and, thankfully, the drunk who'd provoked Saint last night was nursing his hangover and didn't turn up at the track.

They returned to New York later that evening to headlines about her pregnancy, but a political scandal was already overshadowing it.

A small honeymoon period ensued, one that filled Fliss with optimism. She did send her proposal to her potential investor, then flew to California with Saint, where she was accidentally photographed in one of her own bathing suits. Her bump was growing obvious and the rest of her was filling out, too. She wore a seashell-patterned bikini top that tied between her breasts. The matching bottoms were high-waisted and had seashell-shaped cutouts on either hip, each outlined with dark blue piping. She also wore a wide-brimmed hat that she was holding on her head as she tipped her head back and laughed at something Saint had said.

It wasn't a lewd photo. The suit was only partially visible beneath her filmy cover-up, but it was labeled "body positive" and captured an intimate moment between them, so it went viral. All the online influencers wanted to know where her ensemble had been purchased, and when it was identified as her own design, her potential business partner leapt on it, offering her an obscene amount of money to get a line of bathing suits to market as quickly as possible.

From then on, she and Saint both had busy days. While he assembled his team for his security project and oversaw that along with his regular responsibilities she hired her own team, including a buyer in Asia who began sending her amazing fabric samples.

Amid their heavy work schedules, they began hosting

dinners. The first was a fun mash-up of his nerdy program-mers and her fashion geeks that ended in makeovers and at least one new romance. Then, Fliss began finding her feet with Saint's social circle. They attended cocktail parties and galas. People were more gracious now that they realized she was carrying the next heir to Grayscale and likely to be at these events more often. Fliss didn't kid herself that it was more personal than that, but at least she was grow-ing more comfortable in these settings.

The only hiccup occurred when they were invited to spend an evening in the private box of a celebrity to watch a basketball game. The evening had barely started when there was the sound of a brash female voice calling out drunken greetings, but even as Fliss turned to look, Saint was moving between them, blocking her from seeing the woman. He put a word in someone's ear, and moments later, they were heading to the car.

"Julie," Saint explained with a curl of his lip. "I stopped short of a restraining order when I sent her the cease and desist, but there's no reason either of us need to be in the same room with her. Do you mind?"

"No." They hadn't had a night to themselves in ages. She was more than glad that their evening turned into a cuddle on the couch and some unhurried lovemaking. At times like this, everything about her new life was perfect.

Except…they didn't talk about the baby very often. Fliss was eighteen weeks along and had begun looking through books of names. She also discussed with Saint which room she thought would be best as a nursery. He was agreeable but always seemed a little reticent, which worried her.

He was busy, though. He'd been curtailing travel for

her sake, so she wasn't exactly neglected. Also, this pregnancy was happening to her in a very physical way. She had been feeling small internal flutters lately and her baby bump was growing more pronounced, but Saint had yet to feel the baby move.

She had hoped by now he would start to see the baby as more real, but when she pressed his hand to her abdomen in the shower and asked "Can you feel that?" he shook his head.

It was a very subtle sensation inside her, so she wasn't surprised, only disappointed because she wanted him to be as excited as she was. But he wasn't.

"Are you sure there's even a baby in there?" he joked lightly, circling his soapy palm around her navel.

"You think I'm packing on weight for show?"

"Pack it on. I'm not complaining." His lathered hands climbed to cup the weighty swells of her breasts. "I thought you were hot as hell the first time I saw you, but I'm liable to keep you pregnant for years, purely to enjoy this benefit."

"We all need goals," she drawled, amused but also heartened when he spoke as though their future together was a given.

She wanted to believe they would marry and enjoy a long life together, but she also knew the baby would change everything. They would have a whole other human being between them. They wouldn't make love as often or sleep in or go out as much.

There was that other, deeper worry inside her, too. She'd had her world come crumbling down too many times to trust that this new life she was building would last. He might find it threatening that she had contingency plans, and she might have already sat with him and his father as they went over paperwork that explained how the baby's trust would work if something happened to Saint, but all it did was remind her that something *could* happen to him.

She stored copies of the paperwork in a safe-deposit box and opened an account in her own name, one that she used to continue paying rent on her bedsit in Nottingham. She knew Saint took it personally because she told him about it and watched his expression stiffen, but having a fallback position gave her comfort.

Somehow eight weeks of living with him had slipped past and it was time for her twenty-week scan.

"Willow is sending contact details for a real estate agent who will meet with you as soon as we arrive in London," Saint said, pulling her concentration from trying to ignore the fact that her bladder was about to burst. "I'll need two days at the office, then we can spend the rest of the week looking at properties."

He had delayed his trip until after this scan, to be sure she was safe to fly and could come with him, but they were going straight to the jet from here.

"Okay," she said through gritted teeth.

Thankfully, the technician entered with a friendly smile.

Saint took her hand and gave the screen his attention, but Fliss still had the impression he was only being polite and continued to hold himself at a distance where the baby was concerned.

The woman applied jelly to Fliss's belly and began moving the wand, explaining they typically only used the 3D imaging if this traditional two-dimensional black-and-white imaging revealed a concern. She began pointing to silvery lines and blobs, explaining she was measuring the skull and spine. She pointing out the four chambers of the baby's heart.

"Oh, that's a good one." A pair of feet appeared. They were so clear, it was as though the baby had left its footprints in black sand. She snapped a photo.

Fliss became aware of her hand feeling compressed and glanced at Saint.

His eyes were glued to the screen, his expression frozen in a state of fascinated wonder. He didn't seem to realize he was crushing her fingers.

"Saint?"

He dragged his gaze to hers and swallowed.

"Fliss…" He couldn't seem to find words.

She was so touched, she welled up. Her heart grew so big in her chest, it hurt. This was what she had wanted from him. "I know, right?"

His mouth opened, but he only shook his head helplessly and looked back to the screen.

He was still quiet when they were in the car. She waited until they were in the air to ask tentatively, "Are you all right?"

"Not really." He rarely drank these days, mostly in solidarity to her teetotalling, but he sipped a double scotch before saying, "I just found out we're having a baby."

Fliss couldn't help chuckling. "My bad. I should have told you sooner."

"It wasn't a person until today. It was a date on a calendar that I needed to keep clear. It was decisions about furniture and words that Legal needed to write into some documents."

She took his hand in both her own, able to sympathize with his shock because it had taken time for her, too.

He wove his fingers with hers, staring at their joined hands.

"Don't take this the wrong way, but it was easier to think of your pregnancy as a project with an outcome, not the creation of another human," he admitted in a very quiet voice. "Now it's someone I have to worry about. Someone who becomes me. He—" He slid her a look. "Did you think it was a boy?"

They had told the tech they didn't want to know the sex, but Fliss rolled her eyes at how obvious it had been.

"I mean, I'll support whatever gender they feel they are, but yeah. For now, I'll focus on the blue pages in the naming book, not the pink ones. But what do you mean the baby becomes you?"

"Caught in the middle." His thumb rubbed the back of her hand with a little too much abrasiveness to be comfortable.

"I won't use him against you," she vowed. "I know that's hard for you to believe, but I won't."

He nodded absently, gaze fixed on the middle distance.

"You don't have to be like your dad, you know. The company doesn't have to be your sole focus. You can make other choices."

You can love your family. Love us. Love me.

She didn't say it. She was a little put out with herself for thinking it. For yearning for it. They were in a very good place. She didn't want to want more from him.

But she did. Because she was falling in love with him.

"I know," he murmured and brought her hand up to kiss the back of it.

She waited, but he didn't say anything more than that.

They were served a meal soon after, and she moved into

the stateroom when she finished, wanting a nap before they landed, but her heart was still panging with yearning.

Fliss didn't know how Saint managed the time change so easily. He rose to shower a few hours after they arrived, whispering that she should continue sleeping. It felt like the middle of the night, so she did exactly that. Granted, Saint wasn't growing a whole other human, but despite her nap on the flight, she was exhausted and thankful for the lazy day where she only had to meet with the estate agent for an hour in the afternoon.

They had dinner with some of his London executives that evening. They were photographed going into the restaurant, but she was used to the attention now. Aside from dressing strategically to promote fellow designers, she ignored the cameras and shouting.

The next day, Saint arranged a car to take her to Nottingham to visit with Mrs. Bhamra. This was for Fliss, since he was busy working all day. They would have a proper dinner with the woman and her family later in the week so Saint could meet everyone.

Fliss picked up a text from Saint as she was leaving the hotel.

I asked the driver to bring you to me on your way out of the city.

At the office? Why?

You'll see.

A few minutes later, the car pulled into a posh square in Knightsbridge. Saint waited outside a beautiful town house.

"Are we looking at a house?" she asked as he helped her from the car.

"No. You look lovely."

"Thank you." She picked up her saucy ballet flat with its colorful pink ribbon, giving the hem of her stretchy knit skirt a lift. The powder blue hugged her bump and hips before falling to her knees. A lacy white crop top with long sleeves and a scalloped hem covered her arms and upper torso.

Saint brought her into the foyer where a guard touched his hat in greeting. At the elevator, Saint tapped in a code.

"This is starting to feel like a secret location for spies or— Oh."

The doors opened into a sparkling wonderland. A jewelry shop. A very, very exclusive one if the thick glass and security precautions and displayed tiaras were anything to go on.

A woman introduced herself as Ms. Smythe. She had long black hair, bright mauve lips and vintage-style sunglasses with yellow lenses that sat low on her nose.

"Ah. My earrings found their owner after all," Ms. Smythe said with warm approval. "They suit you."

"Oh. Thank you. I do love them," Fliss said sincerely, touching one self-consciously.

"Please make yourself comfortable." She waved at a love seat with a low table before it.

Fliss's heart clenched as she saw the array of diamond rings in a specialized black tray waiting on the table.

"I've prepared a selection for you to peruse, but it's only

a starting point. I can also create a custom piece once I have a sense of your taste. Shall I fetch some nonalcoholic bubbly?"

"Yes." Saint nodded at Ms. Smythe. "Give us a moment, if you don't mind."

He brought Fliss to the table. She could hardly breathe, realizing what this moment was. Her whole body grew hot, her cheeks stung and her eyes welled.

"I keep thinking," Saint began gravely while circling his hand in her lower back.

She looked up at him, wanting to capture and memorize everything about his proposal. He was as handsome as ever, still looking freshly shaved and crisp from his morning shower. His suit was a lightweight sage green, his collar bone white, as was his tie. His mouth was twitching as though he wasn't as steady on the inside as he looked on the outside, and his dark coffee eyes were so compelling she could have fallen into them.

"For the baby's sake…" he continued in a voice that was growing husky.

For the baby's sake.

She knew that wasn't the best reason to marry, but it was a good one. She wanted more commitment between them. She already knew that she wanted to spend her life with him. She loved him.

Oh, God. She loved him.

Her insides felt as though they tilted and glinted, reflecting rainbows through her as she accepted all the lovely colors of love he provoked—the bright yellows and laughing greens, the passionate reds, the introspective blues and the endless fire of pure, white love.

"We should have more commitment between us. You're shaking." He reached for her hand. "I should have warned you this morning. Asked. I am asking," he said wryly. "Will you marry me, Fliss?"

"Yes," she whispered, blinking to clear her welling eyes, so suffused in the power of her love for him she could hardly speak.

He drew in a breath the way he did sometimes when she touched him intimately, as though the pleasure was more intense than he could bear. He pulled her into his arms and kissed her, mouth hot and hungry but tender and sweet. Thorough and…loving?

As the fires of arousal began to catch in both of them, he drew back, rueful.

"Let's pick a ring."

She swiped under her eyes and drew a breath, trying to catch hold of herself. It wasn't the engagement filling her with so much joy, though. It was this feeling. She was in love. She had found her person.

He is the one.

"They don't have prices," she whispered as she picked up one at random.

"This is not a place for bargain hunters," Saint said drily. "I like this one."

He offered an emerald-cut diamond the size of her thumbnail. A pair of trapezoid-cut diamonds flanked either side. The setting was simple yet different enough to be eye-catching. It was stunning and elegant.

Fliss instantly loved it but made herself scan for something that looked less expensive. All the rings were incredibly beautiful and tastefully extravagant and had to be worth millions of pounds. He wasn't really going to give her a ring like this, was he? What happened to two months' salary?

"Try it on."

Her hand was still trembling. She let him push it onto her finger, but it wouldn't go over her knuckle.

"My fingers are swollen." It was still morning, and all of her was puffy these days.

"I'll resize it." Ms. Smythe appeared with a tray that held two filled flutes of sparkling amber liquid.

"But after the baby comes…"

"I'll do it again." Ms. Smythe handed her a glass, then offered the other to Saint. "It only takes a day or two. It's no trouble."

Fliss didn't know a lot about fine metals, but she knew platinum couldn't be melted down and used again.

"Unless you'd prefer something with color? This yellow diamond would suit your skin tone," Ms. Smythe said.

"I actually like this one." Fliss was still trying to force the ring over her knuckle. It was the one Saint had picked out, and looking into its facets was like staring into an infinity mirror.

That was what she wanted to believe, that he was promising her infinity.

"Excellent. Congratulations. Let me get my gauge."

A few minutes later, they were on the sidewalk again, standing in the shade of the building while they kissed again.

"Say hello to Mrs. Bhamra for me," Saint said. "Ask her if she'd like to fly back with us. We can drop her in Toronto."

"It's short notice. She might want to wait until next time, but I'll mention it. Thank you. Um…" She was aware of the driver standing at the open the door of the car, waiting for her.

"We'll have dinner tonight, just us. To celebrate." Saint cupped her cheek and dropped a last, lingering kiss onto her lips.

She smiled shyly. Should she say it? She felt it. Meant it. Wanted him to know it.

"I—" Her throat started to close with nerves. "I love you," she confided in a hushed voice.

The relaxed warmth in his expression vanished. The cool, remote man appeared, the one who only thought in binary logic and looked like his dad and said things like, "You don't have to say that."

Her heart was instantly pinched in a vise. "I mean it."

"Well, you shouldn't." His hard brows came together. "We agreed that wasn't something we should expect."

She wasn't asking for his love. That was what she wanted to say. But she was, she realized. She wanted her feelings to be returned.

And they weren't.

"I just thought you should know," she mumbled and turned away to dive into the car.

"Fliss." Saint stopped the driver from closing the door.

"You can't help how you feel, Saint. Or don't feel," she added stiffly. "Mrs. Bhamra will worry if I'm late."

"Damn it." He should have handled that better.

Saint went back to the office, but he couldn't concentrate. He was snappish enough that people gave him a wide berth. A few hours later, he went back to an empty hotel room and texted Fliss.

Are you on your way back?

I'm at my bedsit.

His guts turned to concrete.

Why?

I need some time here.

He swore again, refusing to ask how much time. Was she staying the night? Should he go to her? And say what? He hadn't been built to love anyone, not even himself.

He didn't even know how to *be* loved. The few times his father had shown him something like fatherly affection had been around things that measured up in Ted's estimation of what was important. Did Saint grasp a complex concept? Did he provide a solution that could be monetized? Then yes, Saint was valuable to his father.

As for his mother... Her love had been a needy variety that pulled so hard Saint had never felt like he could possibly be enough to alleviate that emotional chasm inside her.

This was what he had wanted to avoid with Fliss, this sensation of expectations beyond his ability to fulfill. Of not being enough. Of failing.

And he was angry that she'd put this on him. Was she doing it on purpose? Putting herself out of his reach to teach him some sort of lesson? Holding their baby *hostage*...

He pinched the bridge of his nose, not wanting to believe Fliss would do something like that, but it was the behavior he knew too well from his own upbringing.

Saint and I will be staying at the cottage.

Saint will be coming with me to Texas.

Why don't you spend more time with me at the stables?

Why are you wasting time at the stables when you should be studying?

As recently as a few days ago, his father had asked him scathingly, *Why are you letting that woman distract you? You got what you wanted, so get to work.*

She's pregnant had been his response, but Ted had only snorted with disinterest.

Fliss was more than pregnant. She was carrying their baby.

When Saint had seen those shadows and lines moving on the screen, slowly piecing themselves together into a full picture of the baby Fliss carried, he'd felt it like a punch to the heart. The baby was only the size of a banana, the technician had said, but the magnitude of its effect on him had been world-altering.

He and Fliss had *made* that baby. He was going to be a father. Why was he distracted? Because all he could think about was them. How he needed both of them close so he could ensure they were safe. He wasn't so dependent that he needed to be with Fliss every minute of every day, but he damned well liked knowing he was going back to her every night. Anytime he held her, even if it was only her hand, things inside him settled.

And now all he could think about was seeing their baby. Holding him. Watching him explore the world with Fliss's humor and curiosity.

That was why he'd proposed to her, so they would have that deeper promise to stay together. He wanted her in his life every day. He wanted them to be a unit.

He should have known she would want his heart, though, given how sensitive and emotionally open she was.

Did she not realize his heart was a shriveled raisin of a thing, not worth having?

Frustrated, he paced into the bedroom, noting with relief that she hadn't taken anything more than her purse today.

She must have done a reading while she'd still been in bed because her cards were on the nightstand, not even tied into their velvet cloth. What had she been asking? he wondered. She had told him she didn't ask questions she didn't want the answer to, which was why she hadn't asked about their relationship.

He didn't even believe in these things, but it irritated him that she had said that. He interpreted it as distrust. She lacked faith in their relationship and didn't want her doubts to be confirmed by her cards.

Was his faith in her any better, though? Yes, he had proposed, but when she had told him she loved him, he'd taken it as a personal attack.

From the beginning, he'd known that if he couldn't give her what she needed emotionally, he might have to let her go. Was that what he was supposed to do? What in hell was coming next for them?

He never touched her cards. She had asked him not to, but with the questions ringing in his mind, he impulsively turned over the top card.

Death.

His phone rang, kick-starting his stalled heart.

CHAPTER TWELVE

FLISS'S MORNING READING had encouraged her to say good-bye today.

She had thought she had understood it, especially when Saint had proposed, then things had ended on that sour note at the car and she'd been thrown into confusion.

Slowly, however, as Mrs. Bhamra promised her a knitted blanket for the baby and Fliss visited Granny at the cemetery, she knew which goodbye was necessary and inevitable.

She told her landlords that movers would come in the next few months. She paid them in advance and packed up a handful of personal items, then said her goodbye.

She said goodbye to the person she'd been when she'd lived here in Nottingham, the one who'd held herself back on so many levels and worried she wasn't good enough as a designer or wasn't entitled to live a bigger life.

She said goodbye to thinking that it was impossible for Saint to want *her* when he could have anyone.

He did want her. He'd said it in thousands of ways. She had kept this flat and all her ties here because she hadn't wanted to believe in him. In them. It was scary, especially when he hadn't said *I love you* back to her.

How many other declarations and guarantees did she need, though? He made her life richer in countless ways. Yes, materially, but he had given her a *baby*. He made her laugh. He coddled her and supported her dreams and built her confidence in herself. He cared about her very deeply. She knew he did.

He wanted to be her person, her safety net, and he couldn't be that person for her if she didn't let him. She had to step off the ledge and have faith that he would catch her. That was how she would learn to trust that he would.

So, even though she was hurt, she was closing out her life here for good so she could make a new one with him.

She had just finished labeling the boxes she wanted shipped to her in New York when he texted.

Dad had a stroke. I'm flying back.

"What?" she cried and hit the button to call him. "I'm coming back now. Don't leave without me," she said as soon as he answered.

"Why?" he asked flatly. "Because you think I'm going to inherit everything now? He's not dead."

It was a slap in the face delivered from three hours away.

"You're upset," she said shakily, as much to remind herself as him. "Have a maid pack my things from the hotel. I'll meet you at the airport."

He ended the call, so she had no idea if he would do as she'd asked.

Saint was stewing in his seat on the tarmac, hating himself for what he'd said to Fliss.

He should have called her back, but he'd been fielding

calls from his mother and doctors and the board as word has spread that his father was in hospital.

When he saw the headlights come through the gate toward his jet, he let out a sigh of profound relief that she'd gotten here safely. As much as he'd resented the pilot delaying takeoff—because Fliss had called Willow and told them to hold the plane—he was still shaken by that damned Death card, worried it had been meant for her.

"Willow doesn't work for you," he snapped as she came aboard and took her seat next to him.

"Willow has your best interests at heart, same as I do."

"Do you?" he scoffed. Why the hell was he talking to her this way? Had his father actually died and started inhabiting his body?

"You may go ahead and be an ass to me if you need to let off steam," Fliss said with cool patience. "But I didn't cause your father's stroke." She closed her belt and gave the attendant a tight smile to indicate she was ready for takeoff.

He was being an ass. Why?

Because she hadn't been there when it had happened. He'd thought she was leaving him, and he'd been so hurt, so cast adrift he hadn't known how to deal with it except to go on the attack.

She *was* here, though. Exactly where he wanted her, expression stiff with hurt.

"I am upset," he admitted. "Even if he survives, he'll be too ill to work. The board has already named me interim president. This isn't the way I wanted it to happen. I wanted him to choose me." God, that sounded puerile. "To trust me. To give me *something* that showed—" He couldn't say it.

His father had withheld the same words that Saint had.

God, that hurt to acknowledge. He was *exactly* like his father. And if his father didn't survive, that meant Saint wouldn't ever make his peace with the old man.

Fliss's soft hand covered his.

His throat tightened. His eyes grew hot. He used his thumb to pinch her fingers to his palm. He didn't deserve her kindness and wondered what had prompted such generosity.

But he knew. Love. She loved him.

He was a selfish bastard for accepting it, but he drank it up like rare scotch.

The first few days were fraught and filled with *hurry up and wait.*

Saint was pulled in every direction, leaving Fliss helpless to do anything except provide what support she could. She reminded him to eat and curled up to him anytime he sat down, hoping it would pin him down long enough to force a small rest. He always responded by drawing her closer and occasionally nodded off, but he never stayed still long. He was up early and came to bed late.

She invited Norma to eat dinner with them every night so she wasn't spending evenings alone. Norma accepted a few times, but they were somber occasions without much conversation.

Eventually, Ted's condition stabilized enough to determine he had lost the use of his left arm and leg. His facial muscles were affected, and he was having trouble with cognition and speech. His doctors believed he would improve over time, but he would never fully recover.

Saint came home one evening looking very tired after a long meeting with the board.

"How did they take the news?" She knew he'd conveyed Ted's prognosis today.

"Voted me in as president," he said without emotion.

She poured him a scotch and brought it to him, sensing what a bittersweet accomplishment this was for him.

"Thank—" He took the glass with one hand and caught her wrist with the other, looking at the ring on her finger.

"It was delivered this morning." She had fallen in love with it all over again. "You should have seen the production I went through before they would release it. I thought we were going to have to start our baby-making all over again because they seemed to want our first born."

Saint didn't crack a hint of a smile. He absently set aside his drink and held her hand in his two, studying the stone as if it were a crystal ball.

At his continued silence, her stomach wobbled. They hadn't talked about marriage since she'd driven away from the jewelry shop in London.

"I know this isn't the right time to make announcements. I don't have to wear it if you'd rather I didn't." She started to withdraw her hand, but he held on to it.

"One of the board members asked me today whether we were getting married. I didn't know what to say." His troubled gaze came up to hers. "I was such an ass to you that day. Not just after the news about Dad. Before."

"Saint." She had worked her way through that and wasn't holding any grudges.

"No, let me say this." His mouth pressed flat a moment. His brows did the same. "*Love* is a really loaded word in my world. It always comes with strings. Historically, any-one who said they loved me wanted something, and so ev-eryone said it. Almost everyone. If there was someone who didn't want anything from me, who criticized me and im-plied I didn't have anything they wanted, then I assumed they didn't love me at all."

He was talking about his father. She wanted to wrap her arms around him, but he was cradling her hand in his two, moving the ring enough that it caught glints of light and threw out flashes of rainbow colors.

"I wanted to put a ring on you. To lock you in. I wanted that from the beginning. That's why I sent the earrings." Saint flicked his gaze to her naked lobes.

She had thought the ring was extravagant enough for an evening at home. She wasn't going to swan around like it was coronation day.

"I wanted to give you everything you wanted. It's the dynamic I understand. Give her a barn full of horses and she'll be happy enough to stay," he said. "I told you to trust that I would take care of you, then all I've done since we got back is lean on you. Thank you for reaching out to Mom, by the way. She doesn't know how to deal with this any better than I do. I think she would come more often, but she feels she's intruding."

"I'll make sure she knows she's not."

"See? We don't know what to do with that, Fliss. Emo-tional generosity isn't something we have any experience with."

"You're going to break my heart, saying things like that. This is what marriage is, Saint. Leaning on each other when you need to." She slid her arms around his waist and em-phasized her statement by letting her weight press into him.

"I thought you were leaving me that day." He folded his arms around her shoulders, voice grave. "When you said you were at your bedsit and needed time. I thought I'd driven you away."

"I was hurt and was being petulant—I'll admit that. But I went there planning to close out my life there. I knew this was where I belong now, with you."

"Yeah?" His features finally relaxed a smidge as he smoothed his hand down her hair, encouraging her to tilt her head back so he could see her face.

"Yes. It's not that I don't believe in you, Saint. I struggle to believe in life. In good things coming to me. I don't trust the future. That's why I'm always trying to read it and pre-pare for it," she said ruefully.

The glimmer of warmth in his eyes doused. His hand on her back shifted to her arm as though to steady her.

"What's wrong?" she asked, not liking the chill that en-tered her bloodstream.

"It's foolish. I don't even believe in the damned things, but I was angry about your staying in Nottingham and turned over a card. It was Death. Then I got the call about Dad, but—he's pulling through and now I'm worried…" He searched her eyes.

"Oh, you silly man." She hugged him with all her strength before she tilted her head back to scold. "Don't touch my cards. We've talked about that. Also, the Death card doesn't mean death, it means transformation. And it was *mine*. From my reading that morning. I knew neither of us could feel secure in our relationship until we fully trusted the other to be there. I knew I had to let you see *my* commitment, that I had to cut those old ties, but it was a big step, so I did a reading to help myself process it. If it makes you feel better, the card came up reversed for me, which means I was resisting a change and ought to embrace it."

He only looked marginally satisfied. "What does it mean when it's right side up?"

"It's still a transformation card but indicates a more sudden change, the kind you can't escape or undo. One door opens as another closes. You have to let go of old beliefs and attachments in order to adapt to the new conditions."

"So it is about Dad."

If that was what he needed to believe, she wasn't going to persuade him differently.

He folded his arms around her more tightly and rested his jaw against her hair. "I was scared it meant you or the baby. I don't think I could survive losing either of you, Fliss. I need you."

She smiled against his shirt and roamed her hands under his jacket, against his back. "I need you, too." And she'd been missing their lovemaking as he'd worked himself to exhaustion every day.

"No, I *need* you, Fliss. Yes, sometimes I'm so aroused I think I'll come out of my skin if I don't get inside you, but I need *you*. To say *I love you* doesn't even cover it because I want to pull everything out of you and hold it inside me like air. Like it's something that will keep me alive."

"Did you just tell me you love me?" she asked in whispered wonder.

"Yes, but it's not enough, Fliss. I don't know how to make my love for you as big as yours is for me. To make you feel it and know it the way I feel your love for me." His arms were so tight around her she could hardly breathe, but she reveled in being crushed by the weight of his love.

She sniffed back tears, clenching her eyes to stem the sting.

"Angel. Don't cry. I'm doing this wrong—"

"No. You're doing it right, Saint. You're absolutely doing it right. Now kiss me and show me—"

He did, pressing his mouth to hers with rough hunger, as though he was starving for her. As though he would consume her.

It was the passion, the need that she had been yearning to feel. She moaned with joy, and he jerked his head back. "I'm being too—"

"Don't stop," she cried. "Love me."

With a growling noise, he backed her toward the sofa. She pushed his jacket off his shoulders, and he dropped it to the floor, picking up the hem of her skirt so he was between her thighs as he pressed her to the cushions. He kept his mouth fused to hers the whole time.

"We should slow down," he rasped against her neck, then opened his mouth to suck a small sting into her skin. Beneath her skirt, his wide hand roamed her bump before seeking the lace of her knickers. "Can you mend these if I…?"

"Do it."

He snapped them, and she chuckled with joy and excitement and love. She loved when he couldn't seem to get enough of her. And she adored when he murmured "I'll be back" and slid off the sofa to kneel and press his mouth between her thighs, tantalizing her with one slow, wet lick before making her writhe in need.

She didn't want a solo flight this time, though. Fliss needed the connection that felt so indelible it could last a lifetime. She scraped her hand into his hair and tugged. "I need you inside me."

He rose enough to open his trousers and hitch them off his hips, then he dragged her thighs to the edge of the cushion and half sprawled over her as his hard flesh probed hers.

There was a small sting, then he was fully seated inside her. They both sighed and shared a dazzled look. And relaxed.

"I needed to be here," he said, picking up her hand to kiss into her palm, then down the inside of her wrist.

"I needed you here," she murmured, working to loosen his tie. She left it dangling as she opened the buttons of his shirt, then ran her hands across the exposed plane of his chest, the flat disks of his nipples and down to the tense muscles of his abdomen.

His hands were busy, too, shifting her skirt higher, then opening the buttons down the front of her dress to admire the bra she wore.

"This is new."

"I made it for you."

"Then I'll be careful with it." He played his fingertips across the satin cup, teasing her nipple into rising before he tickled his touch across the naked swell that overflowed the top.

"It opens here." She released the catch between her breasts.

"Ah. You do love me." He brushed the cup aside and bent his mouth in fresh worship.

She moaned and lifted her hips, signaling that she wanted him to start thrusting.

"Shh." His hand clasped her hip. "Don't make me come yet. I want it to be together."

She wanted that, too. But it was ever so hard to let him fondle and caress and arouse her with long, lazy kisses while her flesh throbbed around the invasion of his, growing wetter and needier.

"Saint," she gasped, sliding her hand down to where they were joined.

He rumbled another admonishment and caught her hand, pinning it to the armrest above her head. Then he shifted slightly and began to move, slow and tender and deliciously thorough.

"Tell me when," he said against her lips. His whole body was shaking.

She licked into his mouth in a dirty tease, liking that he jolted and thrust harder.

"Like that, is it?"

"Yes…" She groaned. "I'm so close." She pulled her hand free of his so she could cup his head and draw him into a blatant kiss.

He moved with more power, pushing her toward the edge, then falling with her over it, shuddering and muffling her moan of ecstasy with his own.

CHAPTER THIRTEEN

THEY ANNOUNCED THEIR engagement a few days later, and Fliss began nesting in earnest.

She was still working and would have a big launch next year, but for now she was spending her weeks still putting pieces into place and approving production samples.

Saint was even busier now that he was fully responsible for Grayscale as well as overseeing his project. Fliss hardly saw him unless they were checking in with his parents together or making an appearance. Sometimes when he came to bed, if she happened to wake, she would roll toward him and they would kiss and sleepily make love. It was always as deliciously satisfying as ever, but it was quieter. She was well into her third trimester, so he was being extra careful with her, which was sweet, and he always told her he loved her, but she still felt some little distance in him, something she couldn't put her finger on.

One day, about six week before her due date, Willow asked her to come into the office "to review some paperwork."

Fliss was baffled as to why Saint couldn't bring it home, but she didn't want to bother him with yet one more task, so she turned up at the appointed time.

Willow brought her to a boardroom where streamers and cake and gifts were waiting. They had conspired with a team of parents to throw her a baby shower.

"Willow reminded us that you don't have family here," Xanthe said.

Fliss had met her at different times when they'd made announcements around the baby and their engagement. She didn't mention that she didn't actually have family anywhere.

"Being a new parent is a special club," Xanthe continued. "We're looking forward to welcoming you."

Fliss was incredibly touched, especially when she was given a contact list with each person's professed specialty. "Call me if you have questions about…" They listed everything from colic to preschools to hiring a nanny.

Most of the gifts were unwrapped and wearing only a bow. She admired all of them, thrilled to have so many decisions made for her. She was dishing out slices of cake when Saint came into the boardroom.

"Oh, hello." Her heart leapt when he touched her shoulder and dropped a casual kiss onto her cheek, but her smile faltered as his flinty gaze scanned the strollers and toys and hampers. "Thank you for arranging this," she said. "I really appreciate it."

"I didn't. Willow did." He nodded at his assistant. "I've said many times that Willow is the most valuable member of my staff. This is yet another example why."

Since everyone was looking at them, Fliss joked, "That's why I've asked them to be my birth coach. I already know Willow will do most of the work, and God knows Saint will be tied up with Grayscale business."

That got a laugh from everyone except Saint. His expression stiffened. He set down his untouched cake, said, "Willow," and walked out.

"Excuse me." Willow gave the room a calm smile and followed.

Fliss's heart lurched. "Saint!"

Embarrassed that she'd said something to upset him in front of everyone, she clumsily clambered to her feet and hurried after them, catching up to him and Willow at the elevator.

"Saint—"

"Go enjoy your party. I have something to do." He looked resolute, not angry.

"But…" She searched his expression.

The elevator opened, and she stepped inside with him.

"I'll take the stairs," Willow said, turning away from joining them.

"That was a joke," Fliss said as the doors closed. "I want *you* to be with me at the birth." He'd hired a private coach to come to the penthouse rather than attending classes, but he never missed a session.

"I know. I'm not angry." Seconds later, the doors opened and he held it for her, allowing her to step ahead of him. "Not at you."

"Who, then?"

He led her down the hall and into the glass-walled office that had been his father's. Willow must have sprinted ahead of them because they were dancing their fingers across their tablet, bringing up contacts on the big screen at one end of the room. Some revealed distracted faces, others only showed names. Fliss recognized a few as board members she'd already met.

"Two are unable to attend. Three have not responded. The rest are joining now," Willow said, continuing to assemble the meeting.

"The board," Saint explained with a nod.

"Oh. I didn't mean to interrupt—" She looked to the door, but Saint took her hand and kept her beside him so they both showed in their own square on the screen.

"You're live," Willow said.

"Good. Thank you everyone for jumping onto this call so quickly," Saint said.

"You said it was an emergency," a gruff male voice said. "Is Ted—"

"I said it was urgent." Saint looked to Willow, who nodded. "Dad's been moved to long-term care and continues to improve each day. No, this is a decision that needed to be conveyed immediately so the board can respond in a timely manner. You've all met Felicity?"

"Hello." Fliss gave a weak smile and wave.

"She is expecting and I plan to be with her at the birth. There. Not here. I am not my father, and I will not become him. I want to be Felicity's husband and the father my child deserves. I'll continue leading the charge on my project, but I am resigning as president."

"Wait! What?" the chorus of voices blustered.

"Saint." She clasped his hand in both of hers, shocked and so moved she could hardly breathe. She stared up at him, blinking eyes that welled with emotive tears. "You don't have to do that for me," she whispered.

"I'm doing it for us. All of us." He nodded at her belly.

"I'll continue to head the development of my security project," he said to the board, "but my family is my priority, and you need to know that."

"Oh," Fliss squeaked, ducking her head against his arm because she couldn't believe he was doing this. And she was going to full on start crying in a second, which would be totally embarrassing.

"We'll speak more in the next few days," he told the board. "But I wanted to make you aware so you can start planning for my taking a step back. End the call and leave us, please, Willow."

The on-screen grumbles went silent, and the glass walls tinted to opaque as Willow slipped out, possibly biting back a smug smile, but Fliss only had eyes for Saint.

"Are you sure?" she asked him.

"About not becoming my father? So sure," he said firmly and cupped her cheek. "Do not ask if I'm sure whether I love you. I've been feeling so frustrated, wanting you to know it. When you said that about Willow—"

"It was a *joke*."

"It made me realize that I can say the words, but if I'm not here to show you, then you'll never believe it. Not the way I want you to know it."

"I'll never doubt it again," she swore, because how could she? And she really was starting to cry. "It's a really big feeling to accept."

"Yeah. It's a lot of love I'm carrying for you. Now I've gone and put it on you when you're in such a delicate condition…" He drew her into his arms, hands sliding along the sides of her belly in a sweetly familiar way. His mouth pressed hers.

She went up on tiptoes, letting her arms cling around

his neck as they found the right angle for their kiss. The perfect connection. *He's the one.* It wasn't a whisper of intuition anymore. It was a statement of fact.

The baby kicked.

Saint drew back, dropping a startled look to her belly. He gave her a rueful smile that was so carefree it made her pulse leap all over again.

"It will be a busy few weeks while I clear the decks," he warned. "Then I'm all yours. Can you put up with my heavy schedule a little longer?"

She nodded, more confident in the future than she'd ever been.

True to his word, when she started having pains six weeks later, he was in bed beside her.

"Leg cramp?" he murmured when she abruptly rose.

"I think I'm having contractions."

"Really?" He snapped up and reached for his phone.

While he was reviewing the symptoms of labor online, her water broke. She had a quick shower, then they went to the maternity clinic for what amounted to a textbook delivery. By ten thirty that morning, she was coaxing their newborn son to latch and Saint was ordering breakfast for them. Since everything had gone so well, they were sent home with Elliott that evening.

Saint had just spoken to Norma, who seemed eager to meet her grandson, and made a noise as he looked at something on his phone.

"What is it?"

"I was texting Willow to say I won't be answering any calls for a few days. They said the board wants to meet with me about staying on as president. Dad always kept a tight hold on everything, refusing to relinquish control unless he absolutely had to. That's why it's been so demanding on me, but they want to restructure at the executive level to keep me at the top."

"Oh. What do you think of that idea?"

"I think I'll think about it in a few days." He set aside his phone. "Right now…" He lowered carefully beside her to avoid jostling her too much and cuddled her against him so he could watch their son fight to stay awake long enough to nurse.

Fliss looked up at him, catching a look of wonder and tenderness on his face. It filled her with so much love, tears welled in her eyes.

"Angel," he chided, catching her growing misty. He set a lingering kiss on her lips. "You did good today, you know."

"Thanks." She smiled down at her son. "But does it feel weird to you that they just let us bring him home as though we have a clue what we're doing?"

"I honestly don't know what they were thinking."

They both laughed loud enough to disturb Elliott, who frowned and gave a small squawk.

"Oops. Sorry. Shh…" Fliss said.

Still smiling, they quieted to let their son get back to the business at hand.

EPILOGUE

Three years later...

SAINT CAME DOWN the stairs from tucking in Elliott to find Fliss on the floor at the coffee table, shuffling her cards.

"That was fast," she said with surprise.

"He was asleep before I cracked the first book."

"Lapping Nana's farm a few hundred times will do that to a boy."

They always joined his mother for lunch on Saturdays, but today had been an extra exciting visit because she'd rescued a pair of miniature horses. Elliott was convinced they were his, and no one had disabused him of that notion.

"*I'm* thinking of going to bed early," Saint said as he lowered onto the couch behind Fliss. He bracketed her with his feet and gave her shoulders an affectionate massage. "You haven't done this in a while. What's going on?"

"Work. I'm wondering if I'm taking too big a swing with the expansion."

"You're selling out each season. It's time."

"I know, but you've got the launch of your security thingy coming up."

He loved that she called his military-grade privacy software, which was surpassing expectations in its effectiveness and was already being pre-purchased by governments and security forces around the world, his "security thingy."

"That's all under control," he assured her. It was. Willow was leading the charge on its launch. Saint had an amazing top-level team who needed minimal supervision.

"And your mom has a real shot at a triple crown," she reminded him.

Norma could really use a win. They all could. They'd had a rough year after his father had passed suddenly eighteen months ago, shortly after Saint and Fliss had married. Sweeping all three races was a long shot, but Norma wouldn't be crushed if it didn't happen. Her priorities had shifted these days, too. While she still adored her horses, her grandson had stolen her heart the day he'd asked without prompting, *Go see horses, please, Nana?*

"I love that you're worried about the rest of us, but don't hold yourself back," Saint chided Fliss. He nibbled the rim of her ear until his lips brushed the pretty diamond studs he'd given her on her birthday last year, making her shiver in the way that delighted him so much. "Go big. I'm right here behind you to support and help if you need it."

"I know." She made a noise of satisfaction as she wiggled backward, snuggling herself into the cage of his covering chest. She tilted her head so his jaw was against her temple. "I'm just not sure now is the right time to take on more."

"See what the cards say, then."

She set out three cards. They were all right side up. She tapped the first one.

"Ten of Pentacles. Financial reward. That's nice to know."

"And look at those Lovers." He pointed. "They're naked.

They need underwear, Fliss." Against her ear, he whispered, "I might have conjured that one."

"I know your thoughts are always in my underwear," she teased, reaching back to cup his cheek. "But this card isn't so literal. It represents choice and figuring out what you stand for. Sometimes it means you're facing a moral dilemma."

"Expanding your company is hardly a moral dilemma. It's a business strategy. Your plan is sound. Is that really what that card stands for? I would have thought it meant something more romantic." Saint was genuinely disappointed.

"Like soulmates?" She turned her head so her smile was against the corner of his jaw. "It means that, too."

"I knew it." He dipped his head to burrow a kiss against the side of her neck. "See? Even the cards agree that we should make like lovers and go upstairs."

"I'm almost finished. Look. This is interesting." She tapped the Queen of Cups. "She can be about intuition and compassion and caring. Other times, she's so busy looking into her fancy cup and wondering what's inside that she forgets to look up and appreciate the world around her."

"You've definitely got a lock on compassion and caring, but isn't that warning you to make your dream happen? Not sit here thinking about it?"

"What if I have other dreams, though?"

He sat up taller, then tilted around so he could see her face. "If you have other dreams, you need to tell me what they are so we can make them happen."

"It's something that we talked about at one point, then things got busy. So my dilemma—which isn't a dilemma at all—is to decide which is more important to me. Financial reward or…" She pinched the Queen card and brought it into his line of sight so he could see her thumbnail was drawing his eye to the tiny cherub carved into the throne.

"Angel." His voice shook with the sudden emotion that washed over him. They had talked about another baby very abstractly, only saying that they'd like one eventually but that they ought to wait until things felt more settled.

"It's just a suspicion, but it changes all of this, right?" She set the card beside the others and waved her hand across the line of them.

"Come here." He gathered her into his lap, heart pounding so hard it caused a rushing in his ears. He set his hand against her abdomen. "Really?"

"I think I missed a pill somehow during the trip to Australia. You know how I am with the time changes." She wrinkled her nose ruefully. "And I just feel different. But also a lot like the way I felt with Elliott."

"You know there are perfectly scientific tests that can tell you? You don't have to ask your cards."

"Where's the fun in that?" Her brow quirked indignantly.

God, she was cute. "Fair point. And when have these cards ever let you down? But I don't see a dilemma. I'm here to help with the kids—" He caught his breath as fresh wonder expanded in his chest. "Plural. Can you imagine?"

"You're happy?" she asked with a teary smile.

"So happy."

They couldn't seem to kiss, they were both grinning so wide.

"But I also know that means we're going to lose some of these quiet moments, so let's take advantage of each other while we can," he managed to say, sliding his hand under her shirt in search of her breast.

"Okay, but upstairs. Granny's here." She pointed at the empty chair across the table.

He froze to stare at her, knowing she was full of it. Her mouth was twitching. She had probably staged this entire reading as an elaborate ruse to deliver this news to him in the most playful way possible. To make him believe in cards and ghosts and supernatural forces.

Which he did, because what else was love? Not something that could be measured or tested or proved. It wasn't even a trick you played on yourself. It was something you experienced and expressed and *knew*.

"Thank you for the good news, Granny. Make yourself at home." He rose and helped his snickering wife to her feet, then kept her hand as he led her up the stairs.

* * * * *

If Her Billion-Dollar Bump *left you wanting more, then make sure you catch up on the first two installments of the Diamonds of the Rich and Famous trilogy,* Accidentally Wearing the Argentinian's Ring *by Maya Blake and* Prince's Forgotten Diamond *by Emmy Grayson!*

And why not explore these other Dani Collins stories?

A Convenient Ring to Claim Her
A Baby to Make Her His Bride
Awakened on Her Royal Wedding Night
The Baby His Secretary Carries
The Secret of Their Billion-Dollar Baby

Available now!